DEATH IN A CLASSROOM

A Maeve Morgan Murder Mystery

CM RAWLINS

CleanTales Publishing

Copyright © CleanTales Publishing

First published in April 2025

All characters and events in this publication, other than those clearly in the public domain, are fictitious and any resemblance to real persons, living or dead, is purely coincidental.

Copyright © CleanTales Publishing

The moral right of the author has been asserted.

All rights reserved. This book or any portion thereof may not be reproduced or used in any manner whatsoever without the express written permission of the publisher except for the use of brief quotations in a book review.

For questions and comments about this book, please contact info@cleantales.com

ISBN: 9798316491643
Imprint: Independently Published

Other books in the Maeve Morgan Murder Mystery series

Death in a Classroom

Death in a Prison Cell

Death in Ben Strathfulton

Death in a Small Place Indeed

Death in a Distillery

A Maeve Morgan Murder Mystery

BOOK ONE

Chapter One

"What do you mean, there's no taxi based at Strathfulton station?" Maeve asked, feeling hot and cold at the same time, if such a thing is possible; hot and bothered despite the dead, cold, blustery, rain-in-your-face type of day.

That, she had been told, was typical for June in the Highlands. What had the guard said to her on the train?

"There's only two seasons in Scotland, madam, there's May and there's winter." He had chuckled away at his own joke, moving along the corridor while repeating segments of it to anybody he met.

Well, if the guard was right, she had missed May and was now right at the start of the new dreary season.

Only eleven months to go.

"There's no call for taxis here, madam," the stationmaster replied to her request for transport.

Which is why and how Maeve Morgan, now going by the grander-than-grand name of the Countess of Baritone and Strathfulton, came to Strathfulton Castle for the very first time.

On the back of a cart full of potatoes in coarse brown sacks, two heavy suitcases carrying everything she owned.

Correction, she owned thirty-thousand acres and a castle deep in the Highlands, plus another three-thousand acres in Ayrshire where Baritone Abbey was situated.

"Yes? How may I be of assistance, madam?" At least that was the impression of what the dinosaur who eventually cracked open the door said, managing it without moving an inch from his position, blocking access of the view to the interior. This was the view of her interior, of course.

His accent mangled the words horribly, making it possible he was actually reciting Henry V before the walls of Harfleur.

"I'm er..."

"Back door," he said, Maeve able to make out the single syllable words.

"I... er..." But the giant door closed in her face. Once shut, it looked like she would need dynamite to get it open again. She had no choice but to do as the man instructed and find the back door.

No easy task in a dwelling that appeared the size of a small town. After a few wrong turns, she found herself descending and ascertained that the back door would be in the basement area, leading into the kitchens. Still, once inside, she could explain who she was and ascend again to the drawing room or study, or wherever she chose to meet the staff, which must be extensive in a building this size. As she battled the rain, that seemed to change direction to continually attack her head on, she allowed herself a few moments to dwell on the fact that all this was hers.

"Ah, there you are, you little vixen." Someone grabbed her wrist, a strong, no-nonsense person with the ability to cause immediate bruising. "You're late and we've got a lot to do before the big day."

"What big day?" Maeve heard herself asking.

"What was that? Hark at that, do we have an English now? What is the world coming to when the English take over everything?"

"Not English, Welsh. I'm Welsh."

"Welch? That's the sound your shoes make in all this rain. Sodden, are they not, or me name's not Morton?" She cackled like the witches in Macbeth, which Maeve had read on the train, along with 'Macintosh's Wee Guide to the Highlands', so that she might better know what she was coming to. "Come now, Welch, let's get you indoors where it's a little drier, get you into your uniform and you can start working for your living. We've got a lot to do today before the new countess arrives."

Afterwards, surprisingly, there was no laughter from either Mrs Morton, the housekeeper, or Angus, the butler; just the shrill pitch of Maeve's voice amongst the dead still cold of the inside of Strathfulton Castle.

The only difference between inside and outside in the Highlands, Maeve reflected, was the absence of wind on the inside, making the stillness of the cold all the more eerie.

"Angus?" she repeated his name as a question.

"Yes, milady."

"That's odd. I'm not that experienced, of course..."

"Of course, milady."

"Yes, but isn't it odd that a butler goes by his Christian name?"

"It would be, severely so, milady, if that were the case, milady."

"But you..."

"Milady," interrupted Mrs Morton, "perhaps I should explain. The man who stands before you is actually Angus Angus by name; hence, he is known in this household by his surname and not by his Christian name." This was said earnestly, without the slightest trace of the humour contained naturally within the ridiculous situation. Maeve learned later that his father, also Angus Angus, had been the butler before him. In fact, there had been an Angus at Strathfulton Castle stretching back into the dimmest of past times.

However, Mrs Morton's stress on 'man' in 'the man who stands before you', actually told Maeve everything she needed to know about the relationship between housekeeper and butler in her isolated, wind-swept, leaking, cold castle; housekeeper did not like the butler and the feeling was returned with brass knobs on.

Lunch needed improvement. Maeve Morgan actually found herself wishing for the old days at the Darriby police station where she had munched a hastily put together cheese sandwich during the ten minutes she had typically taken in the tiny breakroom. Everything had been dinky in the Darriby police station she, as sergeant, had happily ruled over whenever the chief inspector had taken time off, which had been increasingly the case. Her sudden elevation to the peerage, following the hanging of her distant cousin, Lord Baritone, for a murder she had helped solve, meant she could never go back to those days, but it didn't mean she couldn't dream of them.

Angus served cold meat. Maeve wanted to ask what animal it came from, but decided against it; perhaps it was a Highland game to guess blindly the source of your nourishment. She could imagine Angus cackling out, "No, milady, it's stoat today," except that the ancient butler didn't cackle, didn't even smile; she would place money on the fact that the smile muscles in his face were rusted and seized-up from not being used since the 19th century.

Mrs Morton had responsibility for the creation of the cold concoction. She learned this through ceaseless mutterings from the pantry she could hear from the huge dining room with its long narrow table so that lover-one could easily stretch over to kiss lover-two opposite.

Except, Maeve doubted very much that lovers had ever

played such games in the dining room of Strathfulton Castle.

"Angus, please ask Mrs Morton to come and see me."

"I'll see if I can locate her, milady."

"She's in the pantry, Angus."

"I'll start in the pantry, milady."

"Ah, Mrs Morton, so good of you to drop in, with coffee too, I see."

"Tea, milady, always tea after meals at the castle. That's how it's always been, milady."

"What? Oh yes." Half the time someone addressed her as milady, she thought they must be talking to someone else. For all her life she had been plain 'Miss Morgan', then WPC Morgan before getting an early promotion to sergeant. To jump up to being a countess from a police sergeant made her feel like she had left a lot of her somewhere far behind. "Yes, tea would be lovely."

"Can't guarantee how hot it'll be, milady."

"Can you two please tell me the strength of the staff? I've not actually seen anybody except you two. Is it a public holiday in these parts?"

They looked at each other in puzzlement for a few moments, shuffling the responsibility of informing their new mistress, before Mrs Morton cleared her throat.

"We're the staff," she said. "The previous earl was a... well, a bad sort and neglected his duties while spending all the money on frivolities. We've had to cut our cloth accordingly, milady. Although..."

"You were, presumably, expecting someone to start today, Mrs Morton, the confusion over identities, remember?"

"Yes, milady, Kat Munroe was due to start as general maid. It's more than I can manage to keep the whole house going..."

So, Maeve thought, we have a staff of three, with two at constant loggerheads and the third playing truant on her first day of employment. Not quite what she expected.

"After lunch, I'd like to look around. I need the exercise after my long train journey, so I thought I might go to the village."

"I would suggest the carriage, milady," Angus said, "except the horses have all gone."

That made Maeve think fondly of Darriby Hall; they always had an excess of horses, but she didn't think she would be able to hoist one aboard the train even if she had thought to ask about borrowing one.

"How far is the walk?"

"Only a mile, milady, and being such a fair day, it'll be a nice walk for ye."

"Thank you. I shall walk directly after my cup of tea." If this was a fair day, the Lord alone knew what a foul day was like.

. . .

Ten minutes and a cold cup of tea later, Maeve Morgan was wrapped in a huge borrowed oilskin, together with a hat that fell so far down her face it was hard to see the way before her. Armed with directions, she left by the front door, Angus heaving and shoving to open it just enough for her to squeeze through.

She reckoned it to be about a mile, half of that along the drive in which the wind attacked her from every angle, and then she had been told to turn left and go along the tiny lane where the high hedgerows would give her more protection from the weather. She saw the sign for Strathfulton but couldn't see any houses. Finally, she dipped down into a hollow and gasped at the sight: two dozen quaint but rundown houses, the Strathfulton Hotel, two shops, a green with what looked like a scout hut at the edge of it, and a separate slightly larger building that the playground outside marked out as a school.

This was the centre of her local life at her new home. She didn't dare go into the hotel alone, but would patronise the two shops, buying something, introducing herself at the same time. She was, after all, their landlady, to whom they paid their rent and looked to for repairs. She had a lot to get to grips with. The estate was vast, so she had been told, stretching over miles of beautiful countryside. She would have to make it pay, of course, otherwise, well, there was no otherwise.

She chatted a while in the grocers that doubled as a post office, and then in the hardware store, which seemed to have everything one would ever want. She left the grocers with a toothbrush and a hairbrush, neither of which she needed. At the grocers, she purchased a big tin of biscuits, then a second one, thinking that the staff downstairs, all two to three of them, should have some gesture from her.

Everybody wanted to hear her talk, just as she marvelled at the accents they had.

"Right," she said, "I want to get back before I get drowned in these floods, don't I just?"

"Well, milady, this is fine weather, so it is." Mrs Ferguson, the grocer, clearly believed it to be sun-bathing weather, confirmed with her next statement. "Why, I only said to Mr Ferguson, just the other day, that I could see the sun through a crack in the clouds. It's just that you English…"

"Welsh, Mrs Ferguson."

"You Welchers, milady, can barely survive through a summer's day up here, so winter will be a proper torment for your soft skin and easy ways."

"I'm not sure it could get much worse. It's that gloomy today," Maeve said, to which the few customers in the shop gave a supportive trickle of laughter.

She left to head out of the hollow, looking at the wristwatch her mother had given her for her recent birthday. Ten past three. Then she looked at the threatening clouds and realised she had just enough time to rush home before the next downpour.

She passed the school and walked on up the steep incline. Then she stopped and turned. The sudden noise behind deafened her. Could that really be what the primary school pupils sounded like as they finished for the day? Or perhaps they were streaming out of school to greet their new countess? For a moment, she flattered herself that they were focused on her and the pleasure they took in welcoming her to the village that belonged to her.

No, happy children shout and sing at the top of their voices. They don't scream and cry. They especially don't shout out 'murder' to ruin the peace of the village.

Inevitably, she turned and hastened back to the school, catching some children as they streamed past her.

"What's happened? What's the matter?"

"It's Mr MacGregor," one wild-eyed girl spluttered, "he's only gone and deeded himself, hasn't he, just?"

"Who is Mr MacGregor?" she asked, thinking she already knew the answer to that; it could only be one person.

"He's only our teacher, miss." The girl broke away and joined the flood of twenty-odd children streaming down the street.

She looked inside the single classroom and found a man slumped in the teacher's chair at the front. For a moment, she thought he was napping, but as she got close, she knew.

The man was dead, quite dead.

Chapter Two

"Make way, make way for the arm of the law."
It wasn't just an arm, it was actually the whole of a rather oversized policeman who waddled into the classroom fifteen minutes later. As a police sergeant, Maeve had insisted on a certain degree of fitness amongst her team; nothing over the top, just a reasonable level, giving one the ability to spring about the place and chase the robbers, or, at least, the occasional shoplifter or petty hoodlum because, apart from the murders that had happened at Darriby with remarkable frequency, there wasn't a lot going on back on her old patch.

"And what have we here?" The policeman spoke in clichés, something that delighted Maeve when he introduced himself as PC Cyril Clarke. In her book, he would forever be PC Cliché Clarke, or PC CC, when she got tired of the cliché joke.

"The children rushed out of school," she launched on an explanation immediately, "all crying and screaming. I came in here to the classroom and found what I assume to be their teacher sitting at his desk. I checked for a pulse and..."

"You touched the body?" This question asked in a way that made Maeve pause for a moment to look at the corpulent policeman.

"Yes, it's standard procedure to check for a pulse."

"I think, madam," the corpulent policeman said, while stepping back from the body and stumbling on a child's chair which, next to the contender for the fattest policemen in the land, looked like it had been taken from a doll's house. "I think, madam, perhaps I should be the one to decide on standard procedure. Now," he pulled out his notebook from his tunic pocket and licked the end of his pencil, thus reinforcing his clichéd approach to the world he found himself in, "let's start with your name and address, if I may."

"Of course, officer. It's... the Countess of Baritone and Strathfulton. My main home, I suppose, is Strathfulton Castle..."

"Just a minute. You're the new owner? The new...?"

"I am, for my sins."

"Then you must be related to Lord Baritone."

"Yes, he was a distant cousin but, don't worry, constable, crime doesn't run in the blood, you know."

"Still..., I mean, yes, of course, milady. It's just that I thought the new earl would be a Scot."

"I'm not an earl, but a countess, and I happen to be Welsh,

so I'm a cousin of sorts, a fellow Celt. I've only just arrived this morning. Come up from Cardiff, so I have."

"Yes, yes, I get all that, milady, but what have we got here?" This, to Maeve, seemed to be going around in circles with the same question he had asked on first entering; she wished for a moment she was back in uniform, able to inject some urgency into the situation.

After all, there was a dead body sitting right in front of them, looking to all the world as if he were bent over the homework as he marked it. There was always the possibility of an accident, of course, except people didn't usually get stabbed under the ribs by accident, especially with the knife twisted up to the heart to make sure the job was done properly.

This was murder.

"It's probably natural causes," PC Clarke said, more looking at Maeve than the body, yet she sensed it wasn't anything to do with her being overly fascinating to this round-as-a-ball policeman.

"Constable, look at the body, can't you just?"

"I'd... um... I'd prefer not to. It's just..."

"You don't like dead bodies, do you?"

"So, what if I don't, milady? It's not as if you'd know anything about the problem I have. It's a proper condition, milady, talked about by the highest doctors in the land."

"As a matter of fact, I do, Clarke. You see, before my elevation to the peerage, I was a police sergeant, wasn't I just? I had someone else with a similar issue and we helped him by a process of gradual association. It's quite an interesting project, actually. To start with, you…"

"Oh, I see, milady…," but he never finished whatever form of sarcasm she sensed he had launched into. The nausea he evidently felt around dead bodies overpowered him, leaving him little choice but to rush for the exit; Maeve felt the wind created by this massive body moving through the air at speed, knowing it was somewhat similar to why storms happened and aeroplanes took to the skies.

Five minutes later, the man returned at a more stately pace, reinforcing Maeve's sense of extreme reluctance to recognise that a dead body occupied the room, that Mr MacGregor was no longer of this world.

Still, at least he had returned. Maeve again wished herself back in uniform; she knew her authority hadn't stretched beyond the borders of Oxfordshire, but she was interested in moral authority rather than the long arm of the law, to utilise a saying Cliché Clarke had already used several times in their brief acquaintance.

"Shall we continue, Clarke?" she asked, smiling in what she hoped was a reassuring manner at the man.

"I will, milady, but you won't. This is proper police work, although I still suspect there's a perfectly valid explanation for poor Josh's sudden departure from this world."

That's it, she thought. Death by natural causes were so much easier to explain, requiring the minimum in terms of close contact with the body. This fat, otherwise jolly policeman, was fooling himself that the death was a heart attack or, at worst, a terrible accident, because it would be so much more bearable that way.

She would leave the man to his delusion. She nodded agreement to his instruction and retreated down the central aisle between the desks, now totally absent of all children. At the door that gave access to the tiny foyer, the office and the main door to the playground, she paused, then turned to ask the constable what his present strength was.

"I don't mean personal strength, but the numbers of police officers here in Strathfulton."

"Ah, well, there's me." She waited for an 'and', but none came. "I can manage," he added, correctly reading the disappointment on her face.

It seemed self-reliance was vital in these small Highland villages. Every time Maeve mentioned an investigatory service over the next few minutes, Clarke responded with, "nope, milady, that's based out of Inverness and we won't see sight nor sound of them with all that's going on over there."

'Over there' was said with a healthy dose of distaste, making Maeve think there was a good deal of fundamental disagreement between country police officers and their big city cousins.

"You could really do with some help, couldn't you?" she said after he'd run through a litany of services that were only available with metropolitan assistance.

"I've taken up enough of your time, milady. You be off on your way now and I'll get on with the proper police reports and the like."

"If you're sure?" There was something reassuring about investigating a murder, something that brought her firmly back to Darriby Hall. But here, despite her exalted rank, she was nothing but a newly arrived outsider. True, she was 'lady of the manor', if you could count that rambling collection of broken-down rooms as a manor.

Perhaps 'damsel in her dismal castle' might be a better description.

This was the sad fact of the matter. If PC Cliché Clarke didn't want her help, there was precious little point in losing one's dignity by hanging around the school, pleading with him.

So, finally and reluctantly, she stepped outside to resume her walk home.

Most of the children had left. She assumed they had been collected by parents or elder siblings. A few of the older ones, she imagined, were permitted to walk home alone. It left the street outside damp and gloomy, the sort of street you would hurry along to get home, a place where everything was bold, warm and reassuringly comfortable; except in her case, she was going back to Castle Gloom, taken straight from the set of a Hollywood movie. She was playing a role in that movie but had no idea of the future, having not yet read the script.

There was, however, one child remaining, standing under a gas lamppost that flickered despite it being mid-afternoon.

"Hello Mrs Count," she said when Maeve came across the

playground and made her way towards the lane that led home.

To her new home. To Strathfulton Castle.

"Mrs...? Oh, I get it. Well, strictly it should be Miss Countess, my dear."

"Hello, Miss Countess, did you see the body? I was the one who discovered it. I was going up to Mr MacGregor at his desk when I noticed how still he was, like. Then I touched him and see what happened?" She showed the sleeve of her cardigan. "It's real blood, you know. Are you really the new countess, Miss? I never saw the last earl on account of him not being interested in a place like this, but, do you know what, he only got hung. I saw it in Dad's newspaper. It said hanging is a cruel way to die. I can imagine it's very painful, don't you think? And why is it that the wife of an earl is a countess, yet...?"

"Wow, you're quite the chatterbox, aren't you? And I don't even know your name, my dear."

"Pudding."

"What?"

"Well, that isn't my birth name, but it's what everyone calls me on account of being as round as a roly poly pudding."

"It seems this little village has a tendency to being overweight," Maeve said to whoever wanted to listen, as Pudding naturally fell into step beside her.

"Where do you live?" Maeve asked the young teenager.

"That's a silly question, Miss Countess," came the reply, which shook Maeve considerably.

"What...?"

"At the gatehouse, don't I just? Me and Ma live..."

"Ma and I," Maeve corrected gently.

"That's what I said, isn't it now?" Pudding's habit of ending her sentences with a question was like a steaming cup of hot chocolate on a stormy afternoon.

Like today. The 3rd of June. The day Mr MacGregor's life ended.

And their search for the killer began.

"No, Pudding dear, you need to get the grammar right."

"I don't have a grandma," the girl replied, making Maeve realise that she wasn't the only person struggling with an accent.

"You were saying?"

"Was I? Oh yes, Miss Countess, we live at the gatehouse, Ma and... I mean Ma and I, so we do."

"You're the gatekeeper? Or, your parents are?"

"That's right, Miss Countess. No longer me dad as he's gone on to another place, you see?"

"I'm so sorry to hear that, eh... Pudding. It must be sad for you to bear the loss."

"Oh no," she replied, "not that type of place at all. He went on the fishing boats and then wrote from Norway to say he had found someone else and wouldn't be coming back. Ma almost burst with rage that day and I tried to tell Ma he wasn't worth crying over. Now Mr MacGregor is a different bucket of fish altogether. Such a nice man."

She started crying at that point, the tiny silent sobs that come before the sobs. Maeve drew the girl to her from instinct, putting both arms around her to keep the fear out.

Then, they both broke into a run, racing each other towards the castle, chased by the threat of yet another storm racing in from the Atlantic.

Chapter Three

Maeve faced a dilemma and there was no one to consult. She had sheltered in the gatehouse while Pudding's mother, Mrs Reid, berated her daughter for being home so late, only to turn as red as a lobster when Pudding managed to get a word in edgeways and introduce her to her new employer.

"Ma, this is Miss Countess."

"I don't care what she's counting, naughty stop-outs, I shouldn't wonder."

"No, Ma, you see she's the new countess, taking over from Lord Baritone, who never bothered to come here, anyway."

"Now, young lady, I won't have you spinning tails in the hope of getting out of your punishment. And, I certainly won't have you talking about your... eh, your old earl when he's barely six-foot under."

"No, Ma..."

"Perhaps I can explain, don't you think?" Maeve offered up, thinking she had to step in to save her new friend from a threatened beating. That's when Mrs Reid calmed down long-enough to take in the rich, fashionable wardrobe Maeve wore under the oilskin she had peeled off in the tiny entrance hall to the gatehouse. She calmed down but immediately did the lobster thing like the red-hot glow of a pressing iron coming off the stove top.

"Can it really be?" Mrs Reid asked when it sank in. "I mean, I heard the new owner was a lady, but never imagined her to be such a pretty one and that's no mistake."

"It's very nice of you to say that," Maeve replied, "but you don't need..."

"It's no more than the truth," Pudding interrupted, "because you are very pretty, Miss Countess."

"Lilias," said her mother, "what have I taught you about telling the truth always. I mean. Oh, I don't know what I mean any longer. Can we maybe start all over again, milady?"

"I would like that, Mrs Reid, if you're a mind to winding the film back to the start."

Maeve had to retract that statement a moment later when Pudding, more properly known as Lilias, informed her that her mother had never been to see the moving pictures and that they had only bought a radio the year before last.

Maeve liked Pudding and her mother, even more so when Pudding let it be known that her ma had never actually beaten her once in her thirteen years. She ruled their tiny household by threats, without the remotest chance of carrying out any of them.

"She's all talk," Pudding said as, storm over, she walked with Maeve to within sight of the front door to her castle. Maeve returned the favour by watching Pudding as she returned down the drive, only turning back when she saw her young friend disappear through the door, no doubt for another scolding.

Her turning around, of course, led directly to her dilemma. Should she attempt entry through the fairy-story high front door that sounded like a wounded animal when opened? Or should she attempt another route into the house, the kitchens, perhaps, like before?

This decision was taken from her in the moment of her hesitation, with the door opening just a crack to reveal the bowed figure of Angus, the butler.

"Yes?" Could it be he had forgotten who she was?

"I've come, I mmm...mean to..." What had gotten over her? This was her house.

"Back door," he broke into her hesitant sentence. Surely it wasn't to be this morning's rigmarole all over again?

"No, Angus, I am the new countess and I desire to enter and exit my own castle through my own front door."

No movement, nothing at all. Her newfound courage dripped out of her like oil from a poorly maintained motor car.

Then, the door creaked open, amazingly going to full width, with Angus shuffling backwards to allow her to come in.

She had regained entry to her castle. What is more, she had done it through her front door.

"Such a dreadful thing to happen today," she said as she came into her home.

"You mean Mr MacGregor, milady?" At least, that's what she thought he said, for the words jumbled themselves together, as if runners milling around at the start of a race, all jostling to be first away when the pistol cracked out.

"Yes, so sad."

"I warmed him, milady."

"You warmed him?"

"Nay, milady, I bid him take heed." So, this ancient old man, who might have served Noah on his ark, had foretold the murder?

"Tell me about it, Angus."

"About what, milady?"

"Your warning to Mr MacGregor, of course."

"Why, milady, has something happened to Mr MacGregor, whoever that man might be?"

"It doesn't matter," she sighed, wondering what to say or do next with her butler, having never before been remotely close to having a butler. What would Lady Darriby-Jones do or ask for?

"I'll have a pink gin in the... yes, in the library."

"Milady, there are some problems with that."

Maeve ended up with a compromise. Despite having 6,000 acres of forestry on her 30,000 plus acre estate, it seemed there was only enough wood to light one fire each day, and Mrs Morton had selected the drawing room.

And then there was the total absence of gin. But tiredness can aid compromise and she was happy enough with a glass of watered-down whisky in front of a spluttering fire in the drawing room. It gave a modicum of heat that kept her huddled close to the flames, lest any should inadvertently escape.

The whisky hadn't been brought in by Angus at all. Mrs Morton carried it in, saying she wanted to have a word with her ladyship, if that wasn't too much trouble.

"Not at all, Mrs Morton, take a seat."

"If it's all the same to you, milady, I prefer to stand, to recognise the difference in rank, as it were."

"Alright, Mrs Morton," Maeve responded but thinking why turn down a little comfort; was it not the job of every human being to find a drop of comfort where they can? What did that bode for her relationship with the housekeeper, hiding behind a mixture of formality and humility?

"The girl from the agency in Glasgow hasn't turned up yet, milady, and, if she does tonight or tomorrow, I've a mind to send her straight back, milady."

"But, just at lunchtime, you were mentioning how much trouble it was to run such a large house all on your own."

"Yes, but you see, we have someone now."

"Splendid."

"She's from the village and you might want to meet her before you give a casual verdict on her."

"Well, where is she and what's to stop me meeting her right now, so I will?"

"I've got her waiting at the door, milady. Shall I call her in? It's just that I want to warn you, milady, she's not exactly maid material."

Maeve wanted to say that she would be the judge of that, but she held her tongue, waving her finger to indicate for the new maid to be told to enter.

Mrs Morton went out of the room and returned a moment later with a figure that made Maeve stop and stare, although that wasn't quite right as she hadn't been going anywhere in order to stop.

But the staring bit was exactly as described. First, the new maid was diminutive. Second, she looked like she had been dragged through the thickest of hedges backwards, then taken back around and dragged through again. Her wispy hair looked like it had never seen a pair of scissors, while the uniform was several sizes too large.

"Curtsey for your mistress, Kat," Mrs Morton said, then explained that Kat Oliver was a little on the simple side.

One thing is for sure, Maeve thought as she smiled at her

latest employee; she certainly does not know how to curtsey, or to stand still, for that matter.

"Kat is a nice name," Maeve said. "It makes me think of the Highlands."

"Kat's from an outlying croft, but she's been living in the village since her parents died in a fire at their home. She's bumbled around from job to job these last few months, but she doesn't quite get along at any of them. I told her I'd give her a try, but if she's unsightly to you, milady, I'll have her out of the door immediately."

Maeve looked at Kat and smiled. Kat smiled back and Maeve suddenly saw a beauty that she would never have predicted before. She felt like Dr Livingstone stumbling through the brush, turning a corner and seeing the Victoria Falls in all their glory.

"She'll do fine as my lady's maid," Maeve said.

"I beg your pardon, milady, I thought to keep her in the sculleries, at least this first ten years or so. I couldn't have her wandering about the house and frightening everybody."

"There's nothing a good wash and haircut wouldn't put right," Maeve replied, "and a uniform that fits. Is there a seamstress in the village?"

"Yes, milady, old Mrs Allison."

"Bid her come to the castle first thing tomorrow. I have need of her services."

"Yes, milady. Come along now, Kat, we've got work to do in the kitchens."

Mrs Morton curtsied and Kat followed suit, although nothing like as precise as the old housekeeper had been.

"Wait a moment," Maeve called out when they had retreated, almost to the door, Mrs Morton stepping backwards as if they were in the presence of royalty.

Instead of two rungs down the social ladder.

"I would have Kat stay with me awhile, so I might get to know her a little." She told herself to stop sounding so pompous and compensated with the friendliest of smiles that penetrated across the frigid room.

"Of course, milady, shall I stay too?"

"No, thank you, Mrs Morton. I'm sure there's a hundred things you need to get on with."

The door opened from within and closed from without. Maeve was left alone with the latest addition to her household, the odd-looking Kat Oliver.

"Tell me about what happened at home," Maeve said, beckoning for Kat to come closer to the fire, then thinking that callous in the extreme, so she rose and met her halfway instead.

The story Kat told was deeply sad. The fire in their little croft had been the Christmas Day before last, started, she thought, but wasn't sure, by Davy, her little brother, when he knocked over a lantern and it caught the curtains alight. Nobody had survived other than Kat: two parents, a grandmother and four siblings had been burnt alive.

Or suffocated by the smoke.

"How come you weren't caught like the others?" Maeve asked, then wished immediately that she hadn't done so. Kat, in reply, slid the buttons on her uniform dress, stepped out of it, and then her slips and petticoats, to reveal the most awful burns across a lot of her body.

This was a slip of a lass she needed to take in her arms, to do whatever she could to aid in the girl's recovery.

"Thank you, Kat," she said as if born to the role rather than coming to it just a few weeks earlier. "You may go now."

"Milady, there is something else," Kat said, just as the gong went for supper, resulting in a look of panic on her face, "oh, I must go." That startled Maeve, but not as much as the realisation that Kat had only the lightest of Scottish accents, really just a burr. That was definitely something to investigate one of these days.

But first things first.

"What did you want to say, Kat?"

"Just that, well, if you'll excuse the impatience, milady."

"Impatience? Ah, you must mean impertinence."

"That's the one, milady. It's just I think I might know who the murderer is."

Chapter Four

"*A* wis warnit', milady," Kat said in reply to the look of enquiry that inevitably followed the revelation of Kat's knowledge as to who had murdered Mr MacGregor, the school teacher.

"I have to say pardon, do I not?" Could she have been wrong about Kat's accent? Had she been putting on her soft burr and now resorted back to a natural state? She would have to find time to delve into that more, but right now she desperately wanted to know who had killed Mr MacGregor.

"That's what the children were saying Mr MacGregor had said before he died." Ah, so that cleared up the mystery of the accent; Kat had adopted a Scottish accent to utter those particular words with authority.

However, it did nothing to sort out the mystery of what those words meant. She asked for a translation.

"Oh, I'm sorry, milady, it means, 'I was warned', but, milady, Mrs Morton impressed upon me the most severe consequences of being late and there's the supper gong going and I'm supposed to serve it to you, under Mr Angus' supervision, of course. The first gong is for ten minutes to supper and I have to be ready by the second gong."

Before Maeve had time to react, she had given the clumsiest of curtseys and disappeared from the drawing room. Maeve looked at herself in the mirror above the fireplace.

"My goodness, I haven't even changed," she said to herself. She was tempted to attend supper in her day clothes, but a moment's thought told her that wasn't the best way to start out with the staff. She had an example to set.

But she would have to do it on her own, with Kat tied up in the pantry, no doubt receiving quite a scolding into the bargain. Still, she had always managed before. A title didn't make that much difference to dress standards; jewellery, yes, with a collection of delightful pieces sent to her by her cousin's executor, but Miss Maeve Morgan had always dressed elegantly, and the Countess of Strathfulton and Baritone would maintain those standards.

Ten minutes later, and only two minutes after the second gong, she stood near the fire in the drawing room, shivering in a sleeveless red evening dress, made for her in an exclusive London dressmakers. It was the first time on since the final fitting and the stiff folds made her feel self-conscious as Angus glided in and announced that supper was served.

"Thank you, Angus," she said with a tone to match the stiffness of her dress.

"Shall I delay it for you, milady, to give you time to change?" It took several attempts for Maeve to get the drift of what Angus was saying, a few more to ascertain the reason for his suggestion.

It seemed that the countess, whoever occupied that particular role at the time, always wore the family tartan in the evenings, with a range of dresses already in her wardrobe.

Moreover, no one had told her, she reflected, as she went upstairs to change once more.

Feeling even more self-conscious, she made her way back to the drawing room, into which Angus came a few minutes later to announce that supper was now served.

Cold roast venison was not her favourite meal. Feeling cross with both of the senior members of the household, she asked Mrs Morton to send Kat up to her room.

"Kat is occupied in the scullery, milady. Plates and dishes and spoons don't clean themselves, milady. I shall attend to you this evening, milady."

"It's alright, Mrs Morton, I can manage on my own."

"I wouldn't dream of it," the old housekeeper replied. "You go up, milady, and I'll be up immediately after I've checked on the scullery maid."

As Maeve ascended the broad staircase, she reflected that a lot of change had to happen if this was going to be her home. She would plan it all as she lay in bed shortly.

She didn't, however, because she fell asleep instantly. As

soon as her head touched the pillow, she was off to a land without Angus.

And most certainly, without a Mrs Morton.

The next day started with Mrs Morton bringing a lukewarm cup of tea; as soon as Maeve woke to the curtains being pulled back on a glorious blue-sky day, she suspected that most of the tea had spilt into the saucer and been tipped back into the cup. The stain on the saucer gave this away as the ploy Mrs Morton had adopted.

"Good morning, milady."

"Good morning, Mrs Morton, I must say something, must I not?"

"What's that, milady?" But Maeve got the impression that the dragon of a housekeeper had expected her to raise a particular subject and was prepared for it.

"I think you are too senior to attend to me and my wardrobe. I thought Kat might..."

"Impossible, milady, you see young Kat needs proper monitoring and I couldn't let her loose on you, milady, at least not until I'm sure about her. She only started here yesterday, milady, and she comes with a bit of a reputation."

These words were said with such firmness that Maeve decided to retreat and circle around for a different form of attack. She needed, first, to get the lay of the land.

"I shall go out directly after breakfast, Mrs Morton. Please lay out my clothes for a walk."

"Of course, milady. Will that be a gentle walk or something a bit rougher, so you might inspect some of the farmsteads nearby?"

"I think the farmsteads, Mrs Morton, I need to see the state of them."

"Then you'll need my husband in attendance," the old lady replied, adding that Morton was the factor of the estate, someone with an eagle eye for how things should be run.

A few minutes later, after sipping at the now cold tea, she reached a compromise with her housekeeper. She would walk down the drive and then turn right on the lane to get to the home farm where Morton, the factor, had an office.

"It's a mile and a bit, milady, but I'll sort you out with some stout boots, milady."

The walk down the drive took her straight past the quaint gatehouse with its little towers and spires in imitation of the main castle. She had wanted to walk alone in order to drop in and see Pudding Reid, or Lilias, as she had been christened. She had guessed, and hoped, that school would be closed that day while the police searched the premises and grounds for clues.

She was right; moreover, she got an enormous welcome from both Pudding and Mrs Reid.

"Are you hungry, milady?" Mrs Reid asked, wrapping a huge apron around her waist. "It's just that I've heard that..."

"The cooking at the castle is dreadful," Maeve couldn't help exclaiming. "And yes, Mrs Reid, I feel like I've been on a 'nil-by-mouth' regime since I arrived yesterday morning."

"Well, we will need to remedy that now, won't we?"

"Can I serve Miss Countess, please?" Pudding looked so earnest, Maeve doubted anyone could turn down her request.

But Maeve did.

"I'd prefer you to sit beside me, Lili... eh, Pudding, because I have something very important to ask you."

She did indeed. She needed to ask about Mr MacGregor's last words, knowing that Pudding had been the last person to listen to him. With eggs, bacon, sausages and mushrooms fresh from the fields, Pudding Reid sat next to the countess and relayed what Kat had said the evening before.

"A wis warnit," she said, this time Mrs Reid providing the translation and a little context.

"For a tiny village," she said, "Strathfulton has a lot of tension bubbling below the surface. Call it as you will, but there are factions and rivalries aplenty. Mr MacGregor might have been involved in any number of petty fights and jealousies."

"I see, Mrs Reid. Any in particular?"

"Nay," she replied, "it was something or other, I'm certain, but what exactly, I coudnae say."

"Right, well I have to be off, a meeting with Morton lined up at the home farm. Perhaps Pudding could clear the plates away while I ask you directions outside. Thank you for a lovely breakfast, by the way."

Pudding put a napkin over her arm, like she had been told waiters did in fancy restaurants, saying she would have the whole place looking ship-shape before Miss Countess could say 'ship-shape'.

"Lilias, you mustn't call her ladyship by that funny name."

"Oh, don't mind her, Mrs Reid. I actually quite like it."

When they got outside, Maeve plucked up her courage and went straight to the question that had been bugging her since learning that the Reid family occupied the gatehouse to her castle.

"Mrs Reid, I hate to pry, but does the estate pay you a wage for your position as gatekeeper?"

"It does, actually, milady, three pounds a week and the house thrown in too."

That was generous, yet the estate seemed to be on its knees. Under Baritone's regime, everything had become rundown, yet here was a single woman and her young daughter kept in relative comfort. Her police-trained brain was shaken by this; perhaps the story behind this would come out soon enough.

In the meantime, she had a 30,000-acre estate to explore.

And she intended getting to know every single corner of it.

Chapter Five

The sombre morning cleared as Maeve walked along the lane to Home Farm, as if God above had ordered all the angels to sweep the bad weather of yesterday away. It left a bright day with the blue sky pierced by mountains bigger than those of her native Wales, not that Cardiff had any mountains within the city bounds, but she had been on holiday to Snowdonia, staying in a lovely guesthouse at the foot of Mount Snowden.

In her experience, people who lived on mountains were good, down-to-earth people, ones you could trust. She hoped that was the case around here. While the settlement of Strathfulton was in a valley with the river Fulton running rapidly through, it was surrounded by bens, as she had learned to call them from the guidebook she had read on the train.

Gosh, the train had arrived at Strathfulton station less than twenty-four hours earlier, thrusting her into a wholly different world. And, not only that, but a murder had happened on the day of her arrival. Would the locals think that strange? As if she had brought the wicked ways of the lowlands with her?

Well, she didn't have time to think about nonsense like that. She realised how rapidly she was walking, her legs stretching her skirt as she strode down the lane. Was she really in such a hurry? Wouldn't Home Farm still be there if she turned up ten or twenty minutes later?

To force the point, she stepped off the road and onto a stile she found that led into rough grazing. She had planned to climb the stile and jump down into the great expanse on the other side, but something made her sit on it instead. She looked over the land she owned as the Countess of Strathfulton, wondering if it wasn't her promised land.

Then, she pulled her pocket watch from her skirt and exclaimed loudly about being late for Morton, the factor. She jumped off the style and straight into some cow dung lurking under the fence. What, she wondered, was a cowpat doing on the far side of the fence, close to the road?

Thanking her lucky stars for the stout boots Mrs Morton had put her in, she wiped her left boot as clean as she could on the tufty grass, then raced off up the lane to look for Home Farm.

She found it just as a sharp shower made her pull the raincoat (provided by Mrs Morton) tighter against her. The farmhouse, in fact the whole of the steadings, seemed to fold into the lay of the land, as if designed for maximum concealment.

A stout man in a tweed suit with huge green gumboots stood by the wall that divided farmhouse from farmyard.

His iron-grey hair and stern gaze towards her gave the impression that he didn't take life in any way, but with total seriousness. Most people, while waiting for a boss who was running late, might relax a little, leaning against the wall. Morton, however, looked like the wall could lean on him for support.

"My great-great-grandfather built that wall, milady," were the first words he said to her, making Maeve wonder if he kept encyclopaedic knowledge in his broad, flat head concerning every task completed upon the Strathfulton thirty-thousand acres going back at least four generations.

"And a very good wall it looks, too," she replied. "You must be Morton."

"I am he, milady." His natural pomposity made Maeve want to smile, such that she had to fight to control her internal urge to break out into fits of laughter. She couldn't do that because she was in charge now, meaning people looked up to her. Gosh, how life can change in an instant.

"I'm very pleased to meet you, Morton. I hope we can have some good conversations concerning improvements to be made across the estate."

"Improvements, milady? Why can't we keep things as they are? Why this rush to improve everything around us?"

Maeve was astounded to hear this view from someone charged with running the estate for the best long-term returns for all with an interest in it, of which she was the leading candidate. She needed to make money to pay the debts left by her predecessor, plus the maintenance of a castle where everything threatened to fall down if it didn't have the most immediate of attention.

She pondered the predicament for a moment and then inspiration hit.

"Morton," she said, "why do you think your great-great-grandfather built this fine wall?"

"Well, that's obvious, milady, so as to keep the cows out of the vegetable patch. I expect they were eating all the turnips, milady."

"So, he did it to make something better than it was before?"

"Ah, milady, if yer put it like that, I suppose a modicum of improvement isn't so bad." Yes, she thought, I'm getting somewhere. "Provided it happened a long time ago, of course."

Blow, she hadn't yet got off the starting block. Still, she would try again later; there was plenty of time to talk Morton around. This was her existence from now on. She was a countess and a significant landowner.

And, somehow, she would make it work.

The tour with Morton really reinforced her view that change was required. She asked questions frequently but respectfully, ascertaining that the answer most commonly given was that this was how it had always been done.

A little before lunchtime, she thanked the factor and bade him farewell, asking how often he intended to report to her.

"Well," he said, considerably puzzled by the question, "with the last earl, he only came here once, milady, so I don't rightly know."

"I shall be based here most of the time, Morton, so I would appreciate you meeting me in my study on a weekly basis. Shall we say Tuesday at 9am?"

"Very well, milady, Tuesday at 9am."

On the walk back, she encountered three brief showers before turning in at the gatehouse for the drive up to the castle. She was used to rain from Wales, but not quite the turn-on, turn-off variety she was experiencing in the Highlands.

A pony and trap rattled past her hooded figure. The driver, a middle-aged lady with a mixed look of determination and disappointment spread across her face, called out to her,

"Watch where you're going, girl. Should you even be using the main drive?"

Maeve's answer came too late because the trap had moved on at speed up the drive. She had just formulated the response that if she wasn't allowed on her drive, then who on earth could ever use it, when she realised that she would never be heard, so it became a pointless expenditure of energy.

She heard the voice again as soon as she reached her own front door.

"What do you mean the countess isn't in? Didn't she get my card when I called yesterday, Mrs Morton? I distinctly told that old buffer that I would call around at noon today."

Maeve could only assume that the old buffer was Angus. She didn't pat herself on the back for that deduction; with a staff of two yesterday, rising to three with the arrival of Kat, a slip of a young lass, there were no prizes to be won for placing Angus in the old buffer category.

This lady, whoever she was, had a fierceness about her that astounded Maeve. Was she some aristocratic neighbour? Perhaps someone she just had to get on with if things were to run smoothly around here.

She went into her own home feeling distinctly nervous.

Only to jump out of her skin a moment later when a voice behind her said,

"Mrs and Miss Hamilton are in the library, milady." She turned to see Angus, not a yard from her. How could anyone creep up so quietly? She looked down at his feet and discovered, to her astonishment, that he was wearing bedroom slippers.

"Angus, where are your shoes?"

"I put in a request for new shoes, milady."

"Have they not come yet? When did you order them?"

"Och, it must have been three years ago now. It was the year the old earl came here, not that he was old, you see, but the one that used to be earl, that meaning of 'old', milady."

"And no shoes?"

"No money for shoes, milady. The old earl took the silver tea service with him, saying he would borrow against it."

"You mean pawn it?"

"Aye, milady, that's the word. The tea service hasn't come back and no shoes, neither."

"Dear me, we do seem to be a bit short of five-pound notes, don't we?"

"I haven't seen one of those since the earl before the old earl, if you see what I mean, milady."

"I do, Angus. I think we have what most people would call a crisis. Pray, tell me, who are the Hamiltons?"

"Why, they're tenants of yours, milady. They rent Castle House over by the river. That used to be the house where the heir lived while waiting to inherit, milady. It's a fine house, but rather run down, I must say. Needs a pretty penny spent on it, milady."

"As, it seems, does everything, Angus."

"Pardon me saying it, milady, but it would help if Mrs Hamilton paid the rent."

"That's an interesting comment, but perhaps not one you should trouble yourself with too much."

"Well, with their being no secretary, and with Morton so stuck in his ways, milady, somebody has to worry and ask the right questions."

"Yes, Angus, I take your point. Now, I better go and see the Hamiltons. Lead the way, Angus."

There were a lot of dynamics to this landowner upper class stuff; a lot of conflicting things to consider. She would be hard-pressed to get around to it all, but she needed to do it and there was no going back to her old sergeant's uniform now.

. . .

If Mrs Hamilton recognised Maeve from the encounter on the drive, she showed no sign of it. It was immediately clear, however, that Miss Hamilton did recall the fact that the trap had gone past her at considerable speed. However, whereas Mrs Hamilton was pompous and arrogant to the point of concern, her young daughter matched her for insolence and sulkiness.

"Good morning, or should I say afternoon, Lady Strathfulton," Mrs Hamilton said as soon as Maeve entered the library.

"Angus," Maeve said, "the Hamiltons don't seem to have any refreshment. Please bring three glasses of sherry, if you will." She turned to Mrs Hamilton and issued what she hoped was a suitably gracious welcome to someone she already did not like.

However, Miss Hamilton was another kettle of fish altogether. As Maeve settled into an ancient and threadbare armchair, recovered, no doubt, countless times over the last couple of centuries, a half-empty glass of sherry in her hand as she went through the formalities, one part of Maeve's brain was observing the younger Hamilton with interest.

She seemed to put on a show and a little part of Maeve warmed to the girl behind that show.

"Tell me, Miss Hamilton, what is your first name?" She wasn't sure if she was breaking with protocol, but she was sure she had found a Fiona sitting opposite her. She just looked the part, with her big glasses and her pigtail tied with a ribbon that matched her dress.

"Fi," she said.

"Yes, I knew it." Maeve felt an urge to punch the air in jubilation, but managed to resist the temptation.

"I beg your pardon, Lady Strathfulton?"

"I just said, yes, I knew I wouldn't be long in finding the right sort of people. It's very nice of you both to come around. Shall we meet again sometime soon?"

"How about tomorrow?" Mrs Hamilton asked.

"Mummy..."

"Sshh, child, Lady Strathfulton doesn't want to hear about childish antics." She took the sherry glass just offered to her daughter and stood, holding her back, momentarily to Maeve.

She thinks I can't see her draining her daughter's sherry glass, Maeve thought.

The formalities dragged on for another few minutes, mostly consisting of a flustered Mrs Hamilton not knowing how she could manage with her plate piled so high. But she was always stepping in to help.

Maeve had stopped listening a long time ago, only finally coming back to the present when it appeared that the Hamiltons were, indeed, leaving.

"We'll see you tomorrow, Lady Strathfulton, remember, 11am sharp."

"Yes, I'm er looking forward to it." That, of course, was a direct lie, although it was tempered by the fact that she was genuinely looking forward to seeing the younger generation once more.

Chapter Six

The big problem seemed to be transport.

Or a lack of it.

The Strathfulton estate did own a few motorised vehicles, but the nearest to anything respectable was the van that was used to deliver the vegetables from Home Farm to market.

"Mr Simms has a motor car he occasionally rents out," Mrs Morton said while helping Maeve dress for dinner, and ignoring Maeve's frequent requests for Kat to be allowed to tend to her needs.

Kat was always somewhere else on some urgent task, or not yet ready to serve a lady. It was a fight that Maeve knew she would have to win at some point.

Right now, however, Maeve was more interested in transport. She wanted 'wheels' as the flicks back in Cardiff would have referred to motor cars as.

"Where do I find Mr Simms?"

"Why, he lives in the village, milady. Has the blacksmith's, which also sells petrol and looks after the motor cars when they break down."

It would be too much to expect Mrs Morton to refer to them as 'wheels'.

"I'll go there first thing tomorrow," she said. "How much do you think he charges?"

"Oh, don't worry about that, milady. He'll put it on account and then the estate office secretary will argue about the cost and pay it eventually."

Maeve had heard about such practices, but didn't approve of them. Back at Darriby Hall, she knew Alfie Burrows, while the secretary, before marrying Lady Alice, the heiress to the Darriby-Jones fortune, had paid on the nail every time.

"We don't have a secretary, Mrs Morton, Angus told me so earlier."

"What does Angus know?" But, it seems this time Angus did know, because a few minutes later, while helping Maeve into the tartan dress selected for her that evening, she confirmed that there was, indeed, currently no secretary.

"So, who pays the bills?"

"What bills, milady? Oh, I see, well, I don't rightly know. Maybe Morton or Angus. Everything I need household-wise just turns up when I order it from the shop in the village."

. . .

Mr Simms was a curious fellow, no doubt older than the Grampian Mountains and almost blind, as she discovered the next morning.

"How do you drive the vehicles you repair?" she asked. "I mean with such poor eyesight, don't I?"

"Oh, milady, I don't drive 'em, never 'ave and never will. I just mends them."

"You're not from around here, are you?"

"No, milady, I comes up from a place called Dartington in Devon. Only I joined the army and ended up being servant to the earl and he brought me up here. But that were three earls ago, maybe four, I forget."

"I would like to have use of your car, Mr Simms. Is it in working order?"

"Yes, milady, but should a lady be driving, milady?"

"I was a police sergeant, Mr Simms. In that capacity I drove cars regularly."

"Very good, milady."

"Perhaps you can show me the car, Mr Simms?"

The car had seen better days, but Maeve, doubting its ability to get around the estate, found it to be remarkably reliable and smooth-running when she took it on a trial basis to visit the Hamiltons at Castle House later that morning.

She heard loud voices the moment she cut the engine in the

drive of the mansion. She had remembered to look up the accounts and knew the rent for this house.

She also knew it hadn't been paid for over two years.

She was soon to find out why.

The previous evening, she had collared Angus when he brought the statutory like-warm coffee into the drawing room and asked him a simple question:

"Angus, what happened to Mr Hamilton?"

Angus' face had turned purple in an instant. She noticed he had clenched his fists at his side while struggling to find the words.

"Milady, he's not... as would be said... I mean, he's hardly..."

"Respectable?"

"Precisely, milady, precisely. He always was a bit on the feckless side, milady, but to run away like that. I mean, it's hardly surprising Mrs Hamilton has a sharp tongue when you consider Mr Hamilton's desertion in her hour of need."

"I see," she replied. "Thank you for the heads up, Angus. Is there any way to make the coffee warmer next time?"

"Well, I don't know, milady, the thing is..." his voice trailed off.

"There's a hot plate in the pantry by the dining room, is there not?"

"There is, milady, with a coal-burning stove underneath, but it's not been used in many a year."

"Well, I'd like it used from now on. Please, Angus."

After he left the drawing room, Maeve counted the seconds until Mrs Morton knocked on the door to tell her it was an impossibility to light the coal-burning stove in the pantry. Maeve told her it was to be done and she would brook no argument or disappointment.

Mrs Morton had still been stewing in anger when she brought the tea the next morning.

But Maeve hadn't worried about that, being more interested in what happened to Mr Hamilton. As a naturally inquisitive person, hence her early success in the Oxfordshire Constabulary, she couldn't let such matters rest.

"Good morning, Lady Strathfulton. How nice to see you here today."

"It's very nice to visit you, Mrs Hamilton, although I must admit to being a little cold. Is there somewhere a bit more cosy we might sit in?" Mrs Hamilton had taken her to the Great Hall, a room that Scott of the Antarctic must have used in training for his great expedition, the one he hadn't come back from.

"Not really, Lady Strathfulton, at least not for someone of your rank."

"I would place warmth over rank at the moment."

Mrs Hamilton had complied, but with a modicum of bad

grace, seen in some huffing and puffing as she led the way into a small study with a roaring fire.

"Miss Hamilton, how nice to..." But the daughter was on her feet, declaring she had some other place she needed to be in urgently, "I just remembered," formed a part of her excuse.

"Never mind, Mrs Hamilton, girls will be girls. I suppose they find the adult of the species really quite tedious."

"It wasn't like that in my day."

This was the perfect stepping stone for Maeve to ask about what it was like in her day, extending the information gathering into where she came from and what she did with her life now.

"I'm well connected, you know," came out a few times, but with no evidence given to back up the statement.

"And your husband?" Maeve felt butterflies as she went to the main point.

"Mr Hamilton is away on business, an extended trip, I'm afraid."

"Really? How awkward for you." Maeve had been in the police for a number of years, ever since leaving school. She knew how to translate such statements.

"When do you expect him back?"

"Oh, not for quite some time, Lady Strathfulton." That meant a very long sentence, implying a serious crime, maybe several such crimes, creating a spree. She decided to probe a little more.

"It makes for a difficult time for the ladies of the house when the gentleman is away for an extended business trip, does it not?"

"Yes, it can be quite a strain."

"I should mention..." Maeve paused, thinking her approach wrong. She had been about to mention the matter of the outstanding rent, but decided against at the last minute; this lady was taut and taut people tend to snap.

"Yes?"

"Ah, yes, what was it now?" Maeve wracked her brain for something to fit with the sentence that she had just started. "Yes, of course, silly me. I should mention that I am looking for a secretary and I wondered whether your daughter might be looking for something of a distinctly professional nature to occupy her time."

"Well, I see, yes, that might be just the thing. However, the girl is only just eighteen."

"As was I when I started in the police force."

"I meant in terms of earning a considerable salary. I mean, the responsibility would be quite something with so much income quite suddenly."

She was asking for a cut. Maeve was familiar with such conduct, not, thankfully, with the police, but in the backstreets of Cardiff it had been a regular occurrence, part of the fabric of city life.

"Do you have any idea of how we might be able to introduce some way of protecting the poor girl?" Maeve asked, knowing exactly what the next words would be.

"Well, no, but actually, maybe I do. Of course, I wouldn't spend it, but perhaps you could split the salary into two equal halves and I become the caretaker for the second portion, which Fi might well be grateful for a little later on."

"So, it would be half to your daughter and half to you?"

"Exactly."

"Well, I see a slight problem with that. Fi will be learning to administer the wages and salaries for the estate, hence she will see the payments to you and wonder why."

"Oh, I don't think…"

"No, sorry to interrupt, Mrs Hamilton, but I've just had the most wonderful idea that would keep it from certain eyes. Instead of paying the wages to you, why don't we just offset it against the rent on Castle House?"

She knew that wasn't going to go down too well, but perhaps it was the perfect balance in terms of looking after the estate. Mrs Hamilton looked distinctly angry, but she was a realist and an opportunist, grabbing whatever was within reach at the time.

She nodded her head, as if only slowly following such clever manipulations.

The only problem with the whole scheme was that Maeve had absolutely no idea of Fi Hamilton's capability to work as a secretary.

Chapter Seven

"I could take her back now with me in the motor car," Maeve said, "it will be live in, of course, with a small clothing allowance." That was a touchy subject. Maeve liked people around her to be smartly dressed, but talk of a clothing allowance sat closely to provision of a uniform and that would go down badly with Mrs Hamilton. "All the best households in England manage it that way, so I'm told."

"Yes, of course, I suppose you could eh, Lady um Strath... Strath... Strathfulton," Mrs Hamilton replied.

"You seem a little distracted."

"It's just the strain... husband away, now daughter going to." Maeve felt sorry for her; Maeve was walking on eggshells, but Mrs Hamilton was an eggshell herself, just waiting to be dropped and cracked wide open.

"You'll come and see her."

"Yes, if you'll have me."

"My dear, I shall expect you to both lunch and dine with us once each week. That is, if you can stand Mrs Morton's cooking."

"Ah, yes, she's famous for putting the worst gluttons in Scotland off their food." Mrs Hamilton made a huge effort and Maeve wanted to support her, yet no offer of assistance could be voiced because of this thing called pride.

Pride freed a convicted criminal and turned him into a successful businessman, who then had to be away from home for extended periods of time.

The actual recruitment process of Fi Hamilton was a brutal affair. A rather put-upon maid was sent to find the girl, who trotted in fifteen minutes later.

"Fi," Mrs Hamilton said, "Lady Strathfulton has offered you a position as her secretary. The start date is immediate and you need to get Mary to help you pack your best clothes into the blue trunk. She has her motor car with her and can take you back, trunk and all."

"Mamma…"

"Go now, child. We can't keep Lady Strathfulton waiting, can we?"

"No, Mamma." She was gone as if she had blown away in the sharp wind that ruled outside the house. Maeve and Mrs Hamilton made polite conversation for ten minutes, after which time Fi was back.

"Mary, run and ask the gardener to bring the trunk down."

"Yes, Mrs Hamilton." A bob of a curtsey and the scene moved on. Six minutes later, Maeve was sitting behind the wheel, wondering how Fi would work out as her secretary. She turned to look at the girl, then pressed on the brakes to bring the car to a stop.

"What's the matter, Fi?"

"It's just everything at once, Lady Strathfulton, I mean first Ian..."

"Who is Ian?"

"Why, the schoolteacher. Haven't you heard, Lady Strathfulton? Ian MacGregor was murdered two days ago. I thought the whole world knew." The tears flooded out now, imparting understanding in Maeve.

"He was important to you, was he not?"

"We were planning to get married. We loved each other. He had gone to the board of governors to ask for a raise so he could afford to keep me in the little schoolhouse opposite the school. The raise and the use of the house were turned down flat. No reason given, none at all. And now the love of my life is dead."

Maeve pulled a hankie from the sleeve of her jacket and passed it to Fi.

"Did your mother know about your plans with Mr MacGregor?"

"She found out and was furious. She said things like over my dead body. Well, it ended up with another dead body, and now Mamma has sent me away."

"Sent you where, my dear? Oh, I see, sent you to me, you mean? No, you're a million miles from the truth on that front, Fi dear. In fact, it was my idea for you to come to me, not your mother sending you away at all." Maeve considered it unwise to mention the financial arrangement that her mother had negotiated, more by suggestion and carefully placed hints than direct statement, but she was in no doubt that a negotiation had taken place.

"You mean you actually want me with you?" The poor girl had no confidence. Maeve committed that moment to do what she could in that regard.

"I certainly do." The sincerity in her voice was a good start to that commitment.

"Even without secretarial experience?"

"I'm an advocate of training from my policing days," Maeve replied, "I actually prefer having a blank sheet to start with." Fiona Hamilton was a blank page, in which much could be written one day, but one step at a time.

"I heard that the new countess had spent time with the police, Lady Strathfulton. That's so exciting. I'd love to hear your stories... if you don't mind, that is."

"Yes, all in good time, Fi, but first things first. When it's just us alone, please call me Maeve." She knew it was an imposition for someone so young, but she craved friendship and Fi, at eighteen, was only eight years younger than her. Surely, they could make it work?

"Maeve?"

"Yes, but it should be Lady Strathfulton or milady when we

are in company, even with your mother. Can you manage that?"

"Yes, Maeve, I can manage that." Maeve looked across and saw a smile that said, 'look folks, this is where I landed up.'

The next topic of discussion was more sensitive still, involving Mr MacGregor, the love of young Fi's life and, undoubtedly, a matter of deep sorrow for her. But Maeve just had to know what the girl was thinking.

"Can you tell me more?" she asked, thinking to tackle it in general and then boil down, bit by bit.

"You mean about Ian, Maeve?" The girl actually had a deal of intuition about her which Maeve warmed to.

"Yes, what do you think happened to him?"

"I don't know, Maeve." That was disappointing. Maeve had expected an opinion, especially if Fi was emotionally involved with the victim. Still, it was a start and Maeve could move the dial on from there.

"What was he like?" was the obvious question to ask next, followed by whether he was popular in the village – intended to lead on to the critical question as to who might want to do away with him.

But Maeve couldn't do it. As soon as she saw the tears in Fi's eyes, she put her comments into reverse and backed out with considerable delicacy. She would find other ways to get to the same result; there was no point in putting this spring chicken through the mill when she had clearly already suffered tremendously.

. . .

Maeve's tactfulness was rewarded with a snippet of information, however, something that ignited her imagination when Fi let it slip just as Maeve manoeuvred the ancient car up the drive, intending to park it outside the big front door.

"Mummy didn't want the wedding to go ahead," she said in a pitifully jerky voice.

"She didn't like Ian?" Maeve judged this to be a safe question to ask, but kept glancing across at Fi to make sure she hadn't overstepped the mark.

"She thought a teacher below the natural status of a Hamilton. You see, once, a long time ago, we were wealthy, but we lost it all through some poor investments. Mummy clings to that past, even though she only married into the family nineteen years ago. I've only just turned eighteen, you see," she added as an afterthought, wanting Maeve to know that everything had been done in the proper order.

A little bit of her mother in her, Maeve thought, clinging to order in society because everything else is lost, disappeared in a series of reckless investments.

Could the mother's pride run to such an extreme as murder? Maeve was sure it had happened before. The motives behind crimes, particularly the nastier and more violent ones, were sometimes totally un-understandable to ordinary people; yet they had made sense to the perpetrator at the time.

Crime was a fascinating thing. Could she stay involved now that she was no longer in the police? She had been fired one day by her revolting, pig-ignorant boss, Rory 'Rude' Manners, but the very next day she had found out about her incredible inheritance.

Totally out of the blue. The hanging of the Earl of Strathfulton and Baritone, without offspring, had resulted in a desperate search through the archives for the nearest living relative.

That search had concluded with Maeve Morgan, a distant cousin, but the nearest relative to Lord Baritone, as he liked to style himself.

Because it was a Scottish title, it could pass through the female line. Without ever seeking a new life, she had become the Countess of Strathfulton and Baritone and this was her first visit to her new home; she had not even been to Baritone in distant Ayrshire yet.

Six weeks ago, she couldn't point to Ayr or Fort William on a map. Today, she had substantial landholdings in both these regions, as well as a beautiful house in Edinburgh and Baritone House in Mayfair.

She just had no money, because Lord Baritone had spent it all, selling off the silver when the hard cash and paper note supply came to an end.

"Here we are," Maeve said to Fi as she applied the handbrake, wondering how much brake power it really had. Still, it was on the level and not in any danger.

"My new home," Fi said.

"Your new home, Fi, once I've got Mrs Morton to sort out a nice bedroom for you. Ah, Mrs Morton, here we have Fi Hamilton to join us as…"

"We don't have any spare uniforms, milady."

"No, she won't be in uniform, Mrs Morton. She's joining us as the secretary."

"Secretary? But that's Morton's role, milady, has been for years."

"Well, no longer, Mrs Morton, we have to move with the times, don't you see?" She had played it softly, softly with Mrs Morton so far, but in front of Fi she felt a need to assert her authority with the dour housekeeper who always had a reason up her strict black sleeve why something shouldn't be done.

"And, another thing," Maeve said, feeling the fighting spirit sweep through her, "I'll have Kat attend to me whether you like it or not."

Chapter Eight

That afternoon, as Maeve was attempting to brief Fi on her duties without much understanding of them herself, Angus gave a tiny cough after entering the office, now designated for Fi to perform those duties in. An elegant room, it had large French windows leading onto a vast expanse of lawn dotted with flower-ridden rhododendrons that seemed to twist around as if totally undecided as to in which direction they should grow.

"You wanted to say something, Angus?"

"Yes, milady, I just wanted to check you knew about the games."

"The games?"

"Angus means the Strathfulton Highland Games, milady," Fi said in a quiet voice, looking up from a giant ledger that seemed larger than her. "It's something the castle organises every year, although it's been a little messy in recent years with Lord Baritone being absent all the time."

"Mrs Morton was supposed to inform you, milady."

"I dare say she forgot, Angus, with all the rush of my arrival and then the murder of..."

She stopped then, silently cursing herself for her clumsiness, although Fi didn't seem to notice as she stared out of the window across the lawn.

"Some rhododendrons are in full bloom, while other bushes don't have a bud on them," she said, rising from her seat and going to the French windows, her hand on the door handle. "Milady, do you mind if I go and have a look at them, just for a moment?"

"Yes, of course, off you go. We'll take a ten-minute break while I quiz Angus about the Highland Games, of which I know nothing, other than that they toss cabers around that look like they came straight from the forest."

Angus was an excellent source of knowledge about the games, specifically what was involved to get them underway that coming weekend.

"Normally Mrs Morton is jealous of her responsibilities in this regard," he said rather pompously after half-an-hour in which Maeve had listened carefully and made notes on the back of some old envelopes she found in a cubby hole inside the roll-top desk that dominated the room.

"I expect she's just rather anxious about my arrival," Maeve repeated, somewhat charitably, because the same thought had crossed her mind.

Mrs Morton seemed determined to be as troublesome as she could, putting up arguments about everything. And now, it would appear, deliberately withholding information about the games with the intention of embarrassing her.

She wouldn't take sides between the servants, though. Angus, seeing this after several attempts to launch torpedoes against his arch rival, decided to retreat and scuttle back to port, in his case the butler's pantry where, Mrs Morton had informed her, a bottle of sherry was always available.

On Angus' departure, Maeve went to the French windows, aiming to call Fi back to help on what seemed a Herculean task of organising these dratted games. Instead, she ended up watching the girl, secateurs in hand, clipping the various rhododendrons, although not the ones in flower.

Inevitably, Maeve's thoughts went to the murder, not yet two days old. Could this girl's mother have organised the demise of Mr MacGregor in order to stop her daughter making what she considered to be a bad marriage?

What had been Mr MacGregor's reported last words?

'A wis warnit.' Could the one doing the warning be Mrs Hamilton? Had she issued a final ultimatum and, when ignored, had resorted to much more drastic action? Who was behind the refusal of what might seem a perfectly reasonable request that the schoolteacher have a rise and be allowed to occupy the house available for the teacher, rather than lodging with old Mrs Reid? Who had that authority?

On the way to picking up the car that morning, Maeve had passed the school on foot. It was still closed and she had walked in to find the whole place deserted. That struck her as odd for a murder scene. She knew local police resources were limited, but would PC 'Cliché' Clarke not have at least cordoned off the classroom while sending for help?

Standing at the French windows, she tried to put herself into PC CC's boots, slipping herself back, metaphorically speaking, into her beloved uniform in the process.

Asking herself what would I have done?

Certainly not the nothing-much-at-all approach that PC CC had indulged himself in.

The afternoon drifted on towards evening. Maeve stood by the window, watching Fi plucking away at those rhododendrons that would not participate in the required flowering. She still was watching when Fi moved to the roses, climbing to great but ragged heights against the walls of the library, apparently one of the more ambitious additions to the castle over the centuries, designed to look like a mini-cathedral with flying buttresses that looked impossible to take any masonry weight in the slightest, yet, so Angus had told her, had stood against the principles of both physics and architecture for the reign of six or seven Anguses at least.

She still stood there when Kat slipped into the room to stoke the fire and bring the tea tray.

"Milady?" the young lass said, clearly unsure whether to curtsey now or wait until she had her mistress' attention.

She settled for now, which Maeve caught out of the corner of her eye. Then, for good measure, did it all over again when the countess turned away from the window and smiled.

"Hello Kat," Maeve said, "how are you settling in?"

"Oh, splendidly, milady. I brought you some tea, also for Fi, milady."

"Thank you, Kat, you realise that you are attending to me from now on?"

"Yes, milady. Mrs Morton told me all about your decision, milady. She isn't exactly pleased, milady."

"Don't you worry about that. Come back in half-an-hour to take the tea tray away and then please go up to my bedroom to get my evening clothes ready and run my bath. Is that clear?"

Kat replied with a 'Yes, milady', bopped down once more and left the room. Maeve turned back to watch Fi, reluctantly calling her indoors before her tea became too cold. And, before it became far too late to do anything about the Highland Games.

"Why didn't she tell you, Maeve?" Fi asked, demonstrating that she was perfectly capable of switching from formal to informal as the occasion required. They were alone, hence on first-name terms with her employer.

"I don't know, Fi," Maeve replied. "When the time is right I'll take it up with her but right now we need to get organised. You missed the bit where Angus was filling me in, because you dallied out in the garden much longer than anticipated."

"It's fascinating. I mean, potentially lovely, just needs a lot of work doing to it." That wasn't the response Maeve had been hoping to hear, but she shook it off as an irrelevance, especially with Fi's next words. "I imagine, with the games taking place on the common land in the village, we need to set up a schedule and then get a list of participants for each event. We'll need prizes. The cups and trophies will have been returned to the castle by last year's winners, but there's also a need for little things to accompany them. They will range from books to flowers with chocolates somewhere in between. It's also traditional, if I remember rightly, for the hammer throwers and the cable tossers to get bottles of single malt whisky from your distillery."

"My distillery?"

"Yes, didn't you know, Maeve? As countess, you own the Strathfulton Distillery. It's a bit rundown these days, but has an excellent reputation. I have a little every day, with water, of course, have done since I turned thirteen."

"Gosh, yes. Well, I had no idea."

"The cellar here will be full of it, probably lots of wine, too."

"The cellar? Oh, there's a lot to find out, is there not?"

"It sounds like they've not been keeping you up to date, Maeve. By the way, I've been meaning to say, not to be disrespectful in the slightest, but if I call you milady when others are around…"

"Yes, the reciprocal nicety demands I call you Miss Hamilton in return. Your admonishment receives my approval, Miss Hamilton." That produced a smile from Maeve, while Fi blushed first, her red hair seeming to get redder still, then she laughed as well.

They were still laughing and chatting when Mrs Morton knocked on the office door twenty minutes later to take away the tea tray and complain that her authority over Kat had been ruined by the countess, who didn't seem to understand the complexities of running a house like Strathfulton Castle.

That afternoon, and throughout Thursday, the next day, Fi proved her worth over and over again. The only complaint Maeve could make was that she took frequent breaks, often extended, in the garden, where she could be found with shears or hoe, sometimes holding pieces of string in her mouth, "to tie up the roses so they look their best". Mrs Morton complained about her bringing mud into the office, but Kat solved the problem by placing a pair of gumboots in Fi's size on a newspaper set by the French windows.

Preparations for the Strathfulton Highland Games proceeded almost magically, with Fi somehow knowing exactly the right response to every situation. Prizes were purchased, cups tracked down and vast quantities of tape despatched to the designated marshals who were tasked with laying out the games upon the field. Fi found time between her garden visits to pop out to the village and arrange various snacks and drinks, principally organised by the Strathfulton Hotel run by a small squat skinny man called Fabian McPherson, together with his huge, corpulent wife who seemed the real power behind the throne.

"From the records I've been able to find," Fi told Maeve on the Thursday evening before they dressed for dinner, "the hotel is four months late in paying the rent."

"How did you find out that, Fi?" Maeve asked, looking around at the stacks of paper strewn around the office.

"Well, I came in before breakfast and started to stack the papers in some sort of order. I found the unopened bank statements for the estate bank account and managed to make some sense of them. Your income has dropped considerably in recent months and I think soon it will be time to take a firm grip on matters."

"Yes, let's get the games out of the way and then we can concentrate on the little matter of income."

"And outgoings, Maeve, don't forget the other side of the equation."

"There's something I've been meaning to ask you, Fi." It was now or never; Maeve had to know. On calling at the police station that morning, PC CC, or Cyril 'Cliché' Clarke, had woken from his summer hibernation and told Maeve that she wasn't to worry and that all was in hand.

Cliché Clarke, she realised, was terribly nice, but totally ineffectual; that, of course, created its own cliché, but it also meant she had to take matters into her own hands if the murder of Fi's fiancé was to be tracked down and arrested.

Maeve had been waiting for the best moment to ask Fi about the possibility of her mother's involvement. She couldn't imagine Mrs Hamilton actually thrusting the knife up under Mr MacGregor's ribs, but she might well have been driven to desperation enough to order such a killing.

"Did your mother, Fi, did she..." It was so hard to ask, actually putting the words together was too tough. You can't just say:

Is your mother a crook and a murderer? Perhaps your father too?

She would have to find some other way to pose the question.

"Do you think, Fi, that there's a possibility that your mother..."

Fi looked up from the papers she was sorting out.

"I don't know, Maeve, I really don't. She's been a different person since Daddy left on his business trip. I wish to goodness he would come back so that Mummy can go back to being how she was before."

My goodness, this marvellous sweet eighteen-year-old didn't even know the obvious fate of her father. And then another thought came to her.

Could her father's imprisonment be connected in some way to the murder of her fiancé?

Chapter Nine

Maeve Morgan, or more correctly, Maeve Strathfulton, as she was now known, had a problem.

Mrs Morton had presented it to her at breakfast time on Friday.

"You do know the tradition about presents, milady?" she said, while pouring coffee which was now deliciously hot, given Maeve's insistence on the hot plate being used in the pantry next to the small dining room where she ate all her meals.

"Presents?"

"For all the helpers at the Highland Games this weekend. I'm sure I..."

"I have not been told about this, Mrs Morton. I must say, were I a suspicious type of bod, I might think you out to cause me as much stress as possible with forgetting to tell me things until it's almost too late."

"Well I never, milady. I don't think that's hardly fair."

"Never mind for now, just tell me what the obligation is."

The obligation was a simple present for each of the dozen or so people involved in preparing and organising the games. Mrs Morton could not, or would not, elaborate on what these presents might consist of. Fi would have been consulted, but she had risen early to go down to the field in the village and assist with the setup.

Maeve Strathfulton, or should that be Strathfulton-Baritone, because she had two earldoms to juggle with, and hadn't even visited Baritone Abbey yet, decided to take a walk in the grounds and ponder what she could make, buy, beg or otherwise procure in the course of the next twenty-four hours.

Being a pleasant day, but learning from the propensity for God above to throw down sudden showers on the residents of the Highlands, she took the waterproof coat down from the peg in the front cloakroom. On returning to the main hall, she was fussed over by Mrs Morton, who pulled up the hood and did several buttons and straps, such that Maeve felt it would be tough for her to get out of this contraption on her own.

"Thank you, Mrs Morton," she said, "I won't be long as there is so much to do."

The whole of the park around the house was new to Maeve. True, she knew the immediate part of the garden around the house, the areas where Fi was to be found if not beavering away in her office. She also had been down the drive quite a few times. But, she chose not to retrace old steps, but instead to strike out for the new.

She took a direct route from the front door, thinking that if she walked straight for half of the single hour she had allocated herself for the walk, she could turn back at the half-way point. Since the beginning of her police days, she always carried a pocket watch and she checked the time on the front steps.

"Five past eight," she muttered to herself, "so at eight thirty-five exactly, I turn around and head straight back."

That was the theory; the practice was quite different. She found she couldn't always walk in a straight line, especially when the going got tougher with streams to cross and thickets of brambles. Besides, her mind was not on her walk; instead, however much she tried to get it to concentrate on presents for the helpers at the games, it reverted to poor Mr MacGregor and how nothing much seemed to have been done to track down and catch the killer.

She had been back to the school, closed now until Monday, deciding to take it upon herself to conduct a thorough search, first of the classroom, then of the office and the tiny dining room. She had even searched the toilets, both the staff one next to the office and the ones marked 'boys' and 'girls'.

It was right towards the end of Thursday morning that she found the tiny scrunched-up piece of paper wedged into a crack between the floorboards of the classroom. She had to find, and then put on, the glasses she had just purchased at the opticians in London before boarding the train to Strathfulton; the writing was just too tiny to see with the naked eye:

Eus wis warnit

Presumably that translated as 'you were warned'. She had taken it directly to the police station where, after a lengthy explanation of how she had heard Mr MacGregor's last words when not present at the time of the murder, she was thanked profusely by Cliché Clarke and told she had turned up a vital piece of evidence.

She left the police station, aware that she was running late for lunch, but with the gloomy thought that PC Clarke would probably tuck her piece of evidence away in a folder and forget all about it.

If Cliché Clarke was ambitious about anything, it was for a quiet life. One in which murders were quickly found to be accidental deaths, leaving the local constabulary of one policeman to get on with whatever middle-aged Highlanders did when off duty.

She had been late for lunch and Mrs Morton had let her displeasure be known, although cold meat and salad couldn't exactly spoil for being eaten twenty minutes after the scheduled time.

As Maeve stumbled around in the woods, trying her best to avoid the thickest parts of the undergrowth just waiting to trip a real-life countess, she tried to make a list of who might be involved in the murder of Mr MacGregor. She thought back to pleasant walks in the grounds of Darriby Hall, thrashing out the train of events that had led to the most recent murders, using inspiration but being able to bounce it off the others in her circle.

Here, she was all alone with nobody to consult.

A decent list needs half-a-dozen suspects. With a dreadful sense of woe, Maeve realised that she barely knew that many people in Strathfulton and they couldn't all be suspects.

"Who do I have?" she said to herself, wishing she had someone else to sound out her ideas on. "First, there's Mrs Hamilton. Could it be possible that Mr Hamilton has come back from his stay at His Majesty's Pleasure and found motive and means to do away with the schoolteacher? Surely that sort of escape drama would be played out in the newspapers?"

A suspect list of one was unimpressive, but she felt sure it was one more than on Clarke's list.

She pulled out her watch from the pocket of her skirt, digging in underneath the heavy mackintosh that Mrs Morton had strapped her into, and exclaimed when she saw the time. It was already 9.15 and, looking around, she realised she had no idea of where she was.

That's when, as her loud exclamation echoed away from her, she thought she heard a cry, in fact a series of cries and some childish laughter, too. She walked towards it, adjusting her direction every few steps as the sounds seemed to dance before her, bouncing off the trees.

But she got there a few minutes later. She came to a clearing in the woods, with the most beautiful loch, if something no more than two acres in size can be termed a loch. At one end she could see a waterfall tumbling the recent rains into the loch, frothing it up before it smoothed itself into a mere ripple caused by the wind that dipped down from the trees and hit the water.

There, right in front of her, was a group of schoolchildren. That made sense, because school was off until Monday. Most people that witness a murder need time to get over it and she imagined schoolchildren would fall into the category of 'most people'.

But this was not some form of group therapy with an adult in charge of proceedings. One girl was being taunted by the other six or seven. She was standing her ground, trying hard not to appear frightened, because that would be like sandpaper to a match.

The girl was Pudding. Maeve moved straight into the attack, someone having mentioned that as being the best form of defence.

"What are you doing to this poor girl?" she thundered.

"It's not the girl, Miss Countess," Pudding replied, "it's the frog."

They had decided to go to the pond, as they called it, to spend their surprise day off. It had all been harmonious until a group of 'slugs and snails and puppy dog tails' had decided to carry out an experiment on a frog that entailed pushing it with sticks. To be fair, the 'sugar and spice and all things nice' brigade were giggling as much as the puppy dog tails.

All, except Pudding, who knew from her roundness what being prodded was like. She had taken up the frog's cause, but had been at a distinct disadvantage until this strange figure in a huge mackintosh waded in to even out the numbers.

The taunters backed off but didn't disappear, being too fascinated in their first glimpse of their new landlady who owned just about everything in this glen and several more besides.

One or two cheeky remarks made from a distance told Maeve that more drastic action was needed. She went back underneath her mackintosh and pulled out a standard-issue police notebook.

"Right," she said, sounding remarkably like the police sergeant she had been a few weeks earlier, "I want names and addresses, starting with you." She used her pen to point at who looked to be the ringleader.

"Who me, Miss?" the boy of ten or eleven said.

"Yes, you?"

"Mac."

"First name or second?"

"Both, my name is Mac MacMac." She knew this to be a joke and couldn't help smiling a bit.

"I suppose you live at Mac Cottage on Mac Lane?" she said and got bursts of laughter in return.

Putting her note book back away, she gave them a stern lecture about being cruel to any of God's creatures, coming up with a neat slant on the 'what you do to them you do to Me' theme.

Then, when the group looked as if it was about to disperse, inspiration hit her square on.

"Tell me, kiddoes, what do you think happened to Mr MacGregor?"

"Ah, that's easy," said the one Maeve had been keeping a particular eye on. "We all know what happened to our teacher."

Chapter Ten

It seemed to Maeve to be a flood of ideas, threatening to drown her in theories and swamp her in immature argument. Mr MacGregor, in the course of half-an-hour of discourse, became a secret agent, a Martian in disguise, a fallen angel sent by the devil itself and a desperate criminal on the run, prepared to do anything to regain his freedom. The perpetrators were described with no less an amount of imagination until Maeve felt her ears were ringing with indignation.

The only thing they all agreed on was that Mr MacGregor's murder had been just that.

A murder.

"By person or persons unknown," said the one earmarked earlier by Maeve to be watched carefully.

"Now, really give me your names and addresses," she said, "so that the best ideas can go forward for a prize."

They willingly complied.

Eventually, the tumult died down and boys and girls started to depart. Maeve wondered for a moment whether Pudding had also gone, but turning back towards the pond, she saw her bending at the rocky edge, trying to set the frog in a safe place.

"That's kind of you, Pudding," she said, rustling the girl's once braided hair.

"They don't mean any harm," she replied with her arm deep in the water holding a leaf for the frog to use as a stepping stone. "But, Miss Countess, what brings you out this way?"

"I went for a walk to clear my head and then got lost. I heard your voices and came to see if I could get help."

"Do you want me to take you back to the castle?" Pudding answered in a motherly tone.

"Yes, please."

They set off walking, Pudding slightly in the lead, happy to be in charge.

Three minutes later, Pudding spoke again.

"You're worried about something else," she said. "You see, I can tell."

"Yes, it's these idiotic presents I've got to supply."

"Presents?"

"Yes, for the Highland Games. Apparently, it's tradition for the earl or countess to give..."

"Presents to all the helpers, yes, everyone knows that, Miss Countess."

"Everybody, it seems, but me."

"But why does that worry you, Miss?"

"Because I have no idea how to get a dozen or more presents within a few hours."

"Well, I can help."

"But there are no shops around."

"We don't need shops, Miss Countess. I can make them. Just tell me how many ladies and how many gentlemen and I'll do the rest."

"Really? By tomorrow morning?"

"Yes, no problem. I'll make a start right after lunch. Here's the path to my house. You go straight on this other path and you'll find yourself back at the castle."

Sure enough, after ten minutes of steady walking, Maeve found herself back at the castle. From a distance, as soon as she came out from the trees, she saw a brace of police cars on the drive. Maybe something was, at long last, happening in the murder case.

There was something happening, just not what she expected.

. . .

"Detective Inspector Cassidy," the tall, thin detective said, but offered no hand to shake.

"Have you come about the murder in the classroom?" Maeve answered, withdrawing her hand before it became embarrassing to have it hanging in the air.

"Yes," the detective inspector said. He had a flat voice, slight sounds accompanying it, but coming from one of the nasal passages rather than fighting through the vocal chords.

"Any news?"

"Yes." Was the man going to deal perpetually in single-syllable utterances?

"So what news?"

"We would like you to come down to the station to answer a few questions if it pleases you."

"Not particularly, but if it helps the case, I can pop down after lunch."

"I meant now, Lady Strathfulton, this is serious."

"Very well, Mr Cassidy. I shall come down and help you with your enquiries."

The trip to the police station took only a few minutes by car. Once there, she was shown to a cell, which surprised her considerably. Perhaps they had no more space in the interview rooms. It mattered not, she would soon be home.

Funny, she thought, that was the first time she had thought about the castle as her home. I suppose, compared to a prison cell, the huge pile of stones did constitute a home.

The detective inspector eventually came to interview her. He had to unlock the door to the interview room, suggesting that having no space had not been the reason she had been accommodated as if she was a criminal.

Ten minutes after the boring questions began, Maeve was formally charged with the murder of Ian MacGregor, the school teacher.

Five minutes after that, she was back in the cell, kicking the wall in the most intense frustration she had ever witnessed.

All the time they were concentrating on her, of course, they weren't out looking for the real killer. She had tried to relay that to the inspector, but had just got told that's what they all said.

"All the evidence points to you, an outsider, barging in here and causing mayhem."

Even if that had been the case, Maeve thought, there's a world of a difference between mayhem and murder.

She closed her eyes after sitting on the mattress provided. What would the headlines say:

Heir to Hung Earl to be Hung for Murder

Or:

It Must Run in the Family

Somehow, from her prison cell, she had to prove her innocence and she wasn't at all sure she could manage that locked up with the key thrown away.

What would Lady Darriby-Jones say? She would concentrate on the strictly practical, that much was for sure, seeing calmness as a weapon to fight back, however much turmoil she felt inside.

Chapter Eleven

"I need to make a phone call," Maeve said when a woman that looked straight out of a comic book brought her some lunch. Her mouth hung open, as if the hinges had worn out, revealing one, no two, or even three teeth spaced out around her gums. Deep sniff lines ran either side of her red nose, indicating a weakness for alcohol and making Maeve wonder whether it was still gin as ladies' ruin when one got north of the border, or whether Scotch took over, being the national drink. Her grey hair was in messy strands either side of her face, looking to Maeve as if it had never experienced a hair brush.

"What ye sayin?" The words came out of one side of her mouth, making Maeve sure the poor woman had had a seizure at some point.

Maybe she hadn't even noticed when the seizure picked her out, pouncing upon her.

"I bringed ye some lunch, didn't I?" That was the closest Maeve could get to a translation into English.

"Thank you, Mrs eh…"

"Mrs Ritchie as is." She didn't look severe, more disinterested, as if she was going through the motions and had seen every eventuality that could occur at a police station, at least twice. It gave Maeve an idea.

"Mrs Ritchie, no doubt you have dozens of gorgeous grandchildren." Maeve felt a surge of hope; her instinct had been spot on. Mrs Ritchie exclaimed that she had twenty of the little bairns and they were coming at a rate of two or three a year. As she relayed this information, Maeve noticed a smile creeping across her face.

It turned the woman into something else entirely, adding interest and love to her features like pixie dust. Her eyes lit up and she fairly bounced around the cell, trying to get to a pocket in her torn dress.

"You have some photographs?" Maeve asked.

"Och, I do. Here's one of nineteen of 'em, taken afore young Margaret came along. She's the latest and the daughter of my son, so also a Ritchie for the records."

"They are so bonnie, Mrs Ritchie." Maeve had a panicked moment when she wondered whether the deliberate adoption of the Scottish word would make this old woman stop and think again about her relationship with the prisoner.

"Well, don't let the lads hear you say bonnie," she chuckled and a friendship was made.

. . .

That new friendship didn't help Maeve get to the phone, however, at least not a working one, for the station phone wasn't in working order. Mrs Ritchie, also a Margaret, led Maeve to it, only to find a sign on it informing the world that it was 'brak'.

As Mrs Ritchie led Maeve back to her prison cell, the old woman tried to comfort her.

"There is something else you could do for me," Maeve said, making her diction as clear as possible to breach the language barrier, also wondering if she was pushing her new friendship a bit too far. "After you finish work, could you go up to the castle and seek out Fi Hamilton? Would you tell her to ring the family lawyers, Munro, Dunstan, and Munro in Inverness?"

"Lordy me, I'll do that for ye," Mrs Ritchie replied without a moment's hesitation. "Tell me, girl, do you work at the castle? Is Fi Hamilton your supervisor?"

"No, Mrs Ritchie, I'm afraid you've got it all wrong. Fi Hamilton works for me. I'm the new countess following the…"

"Oh, dear me, you're the countess? With the earl being dead, you've inherited the throne? Oh, milady, and here was me thinking you were a domestic at the castle. Of course I'll help you, milady."

Maeve looked down at her clothes, wondering how she could be confused for a working girl. That's when she noticed her torn skirt and the mud drying on her jacket, stockings and caked on her shoes. She felt a huge swell of laughter rising up through her body. That broke out and, when Mrs Ritchie added her guffaws to the mix, it seemed the police cell would split open allowing Maeve to step out and walk home.

Mrs Ritchie was good to her word. Fi turned up two hours later, insisting on being allowed to talk to Maeve in private.

"Maeve," she said, following the protocol the countess had set in place for when they were alone, "you look quite a state. Whatever has happened?"

"I've been charged with murder," Maeve replied. At one level it seemed impossible, incredible, completely unlikely, yet at another, it had happened and the charge sheet would not lie.

"Oh my, that's what Mrs Ritchie said when she came to find me, but I didn't dare think it the case. I've been at the field all morning. There's so much to sort out and the games start tomorrow morning. Mrs Ritchie found me there and told me what had happened."

Fi did give the good news that legal help was on its way. She had stopped at the Strathfulton Hotel and used their phone to ring Munro, Dunstan and Munro.

"I spoke to the young Mr Munro and he's on his way immediately."

"From Inverness?"

"Yes, it will take a few hours but he's dropped everything to come to your rescue, Maeve."

"Good, thank you, Fi, you've been a brick." She desperately wanted to ask Fi about the one name she had on her suspect list, but couldn't because the single entry was Fi's mother. She would have to choose her timing carefully, not wanting to alienate one of her few friends in the world.

Well, one of the very few in Scotland, at least.

Mr Munro actually arrived surprisingly early, explaining that he had jumped in his aeroplane and landed on the field where the games would be held tomorrow.

"There's quite a gaggle of children around my aeroplane. Tell me, don't the little rascals go to school of a weekday?"

"That's the thing, Mr Munro," Maeve replied, while Fi went to ask PC Clarke for some tea and to find out where Detective Inspector Cassidy had got to. "The murder happened in the school and the school had to close, at least while the premises could be searched, giving the 'little rascals' a few days of holiday."

"Ah, well, I'd put them at the top of my suspect list, wouldn't you? A few days extra holiday is quite a motive for murder in my book."

Mr Robert Munro was charmingly pleasant, good looking, too. Maeve warmed to him enormously, wanting to know more about him. Most men would run a mile when they first learned that she was, or had been, a sergeant in the Oxfordshire Constabulary, no doubt thinking that was man's work. A few times she had tried to explain that the world after the war to end all wars was changing, but when one young fellow joked about chaining herself to the railings, she had decided to give up on the courting and concentrate on her career.

Now, she was looking directly at a man who made her heart miss beats on a regular basis.

Or, she thought, should that be an irregular basis?

"First things first," Robert Munro said. "We need to get you out of here." That statement about 'first things first' could be read in two ways. Maeve liked to think it promised some time with Mr Munro after he had the charges squashed. "For squashed they will be, milady, after I've had a go at them."

The only problem with Mr Munro's strategy was that nobody could be found to lay it out before; the 'enemy' was strangely absent. Cyril 'Cliché' Clarke had made the tea as requested, even adding a box of rich chocolate biscuits. Then, he had disappeared and could not be found wherever Fi and Mr Munro went in search of him.

Detective Inspector Cassidy was eventually found in the bar of the Strathfulton Hotel, far too merry to conduct police business. Instead, he seemed to recognise Mr Munro from some long-forgotten seminar they had both attended, slapping him on the back and inviting him for a wee dram.

Of course, Mr Munro accepted; what wise lawyer would turn down an opportunity to sniff around behind enemy lines?

Mrs Ritchie came back for the evening meal, smiling the moment she saw Maeve, her new landlady, as she was to almost all the houses in the village. She chatted through the open door of the cell, calling from the tiny kitchen as she bustled about making 'Ritchie's Right guid stew', but declining to tell Maeve what meat was going into it.

"It's nae dog, but I'll say no more," she laughed and it caught Fi as she entered the police station again, shaking her head in frustration. Soon, she had lost her frustration, joining the others in the type of laughter that finds new life every time it's supposed to lie down and go to sleep.

There was nothing for it but to spend the night in the police cell. Maeve could have walked out at any time, but she decided to sit it out and be released properly in the morning.

"Mr Munro, can I suggest you go to the Strathfulton Hotel? You're most welcome to stay at the castle with Fi, but I just thought it..."

"Might be better to be on site when Cassidy wakes with a splitting headache in the morning and drag him down here. Yes, I agree, Lady Strathfulton. That's excellent thinking, if I might say so."

"Please call me Maeve."

"Only if you'll call me Robert." That was a deal done.

"Now," Maeve said, after they had shared the 'Highland Coo Stew' that Mrs Ritchie had prepared for them, "you need to go back home, Fi."

"No way, Maeve, I'm stopping here with you."

"You can't. You haven't been charged with anything."

Mr Munro had the perfect answer to that problem. He stood, summoning every drop of solemnity he could manage.

"Miss Fiona Flora Hamilton?" he asked, sounding close to solemn, but with a strain in his voice that said serious be damned, he was going to join in the fun.

"Yes, Mr Munro?"

"I'm placing you under citizen's arrest."

She looked confused a moment, then it dawned on her what was happening.

"What charge?" someone else asked.

"Why, lack of respect in calling your employer by her first name."

"Well, Mr Private Citizen, you have me bang to rights, guilty as charged. What do you think will become of me?"

"Oh, probably the noose followed by a lifetime behind bars."

Mrs Ritchie then took the lead by illustrating how the beds in each cell weren't actually fixed to the floor, just screwed in place. She produced a screwdriver and Mr Munro did the loosening. Then, they dragged the free bed from the spare cell to the one occupied by the Countess of Baritone and Strathfulton.

And the two prisoners settled down for the night.

Chapter Twelve

DI Cassidy did, indeed, wake with a splitting headache, evidenced by Maeve and Fi when he arrived at Strathfulton Police Station around 9.30 in the morning, holding his head in his hands, much as you would with the coveted egg of a rare bird.

He arrived to find Maeve and Fi washing up the dishes in the tiny kitchen, while Mrs Ritchie regaled Mr Munro in the interview room with endless tales of the male members of her family, who seemed to live just about on the right side of the divide between lawful and criminal activity.

"It's a wonder," Robert Munro said through his laughter, "that you came to work here with so many 'baduns' in the family.

"Ah, there's reason for that, Mr Munro. You see, they begged me to apply for the job and were overjoyed, every man jack of them when I got accepted forty-one years ago."

"Because, no doubt, if they were going to be locked up, they wanted to ensure there was a good cook on the premises."

"Actually, it was something like that. Och, here's the inspector. Good morning, Mr Cassidy, sir."

"Where's the good in it, that's what I want to know." At least that's what Maeve thought he said, or groaned, as she wiped her hands on a dishcloth and came into the interview room, intent upon her freedom as soon as it could be managed.

The rest of the release process was pretty straightforward. Maeve got the impression that if one put the right people in with Robert Munro, you would always get the result you needed. In her case, that meant freedom, with Fi trotting out right behind her, the inspector threatening to arrest her for wasting police time, "and resources," he added, "after all, you had no right to eat breakfast here."

Fi told Maeve that she had almost replied, "just as you had no right to drink your overnight expense allowance."

"It's as well you didn't say that, Fi," Maeve countered as they walked back to the castle. "There's no point in making enemies."

"Received loud and clear," Fi said, mimicking the aeroplane pilots of the war; heroes, one and all, certainly amongst the ladies who had grown up during that time.

"Of course, Mr Munro got what I think he wanted too," Maeve said a few minutes later.

"Oh, what's that?" Fi skipped ahead of Maeve and turned to face her, swirling her rather ragged dress.

"A kiss from little old me," Maeve replied, "strictly out of gratitude, I hope you know." The last clause was due to the fact that Fi, still facing Maeve, hence walking backwards, was doing a very good act of a young girl hopelessly bowled over by her beau. "Now, we'll have to get you some new clothes, Fi. I like my people to be smart, you know. Why are you laughing at me? Oh, I see, yes, but there are extenuating circumstances in my case, you know."

"As there are in mine, Maeve," Fi replied, completely seriously now, "my circumstances are utter poverty, although we are a family that holds our heads up high in society, at least that's what Mamma always says. It's just circumstances that have rather messed things up more recently."

"In what way?" Was it right to push and probe a girl who had rapidly become close to her? The answer was given by Fi's next words:

"Oh, my goodness me," Fi exclaimed, "I've just remembered that I left the car by the games field. We can fetch it now and arrive back at the castle in style."

Maeve had little choice but to follow the now-hurrying Fi, thinking she had missed an opportunity to seek the knowledge she desperately wanted to own. It occurred to her that there were other things, beside vast estates, that one could own, and knowledge would definitely be one of them.

At least Fi's remembering that she had left the car in the village would save them twenty minutes, precious minutes when they needed to rush back home to change for the games.

For which Maeve did not want to be late, not with her ribbon snipping duties as the countess.

Then, as Fi was pushing the car through its paces, explaining that her Daddy had taught her how to drive, they passed the gatehouse where Pudding lived and Maeve remembered the need for presents.

"What did you say?" shouted Fi, the wind rushing in through the open window on the passenger side; open because it refused to close.

"Can you stop the car, please?" Maeve shouted above the noise and Fi did exactly that, only slamming on the brakes so hard that the car slid around on the road in a manoeuvre that looked almost perfect as the car now faced the gatehouse they had just passed.

"Goodness me," said Fi.

"Goodness, goodness, goodness me," said Maeve.

Before they knew it, Pudding was out on the road with her mother, both sets of arms bundled up with neat packages.

"Here you are, Miss Countess," Pudding said, "seven presents with blue ribbons for the boys and five with pink for the girls."

"What are they?" Fi asked, Maeve still being in shock from Fi's frantic driving.

"You'll have to wait and see, Miss Fi," Pudding answered with a cheekiness that registered with Maeve later on when

Kat had drawn a bath for her and she could relax for a few minutes before dressing for the games. "Just remember, start small and work your way up to the biggest one as you go from junior to senior."

"Junior to senior," Maeve echoed like a lonely saxophone when the beat and the bass had stopped.

"Yes, milady," Mrs Reid, Pudding's mother, replied, "you see the volunteers who have helped with the games will be presented to you in seniority order. All you need to do is remember pink ribbon if it's a girl and..."

"Blue for a boy, going up in size order," Fi completed Mrs Reid's explanation for her, as Pudding opened the car door and bundled the presents she carried onto the spacious back seat, then took those her mother carried and deposited them as well.

"I wrapped the girls presents and Mamma wrapped the boy ones. I took special care over the bows, you see, to make them just right."

Fi, noticing Maeve was still in shock, did the required thing in getting out of the car and inspecting the presents. "Yes, beautifully wrapped, Pudding," she said. "I can see that you put in a lot of effort and I'm so excited to see what you've chosen for them."

That happened to be the perfect response, evidenced in the broad smile on Pudding's round face, even broader when Fi went one step further and asked Pudding, on behalf of Maeve, whether she would be kind enough to attend the opening ceremony and hand each present to the countess one at a time, "to ensure no mistakes."

"Oh, how wonderful," Pudding replied, "Miss Fi, I'd be delighted. What a responsibility."

"Well, come along now," her mother said, not being able to hide her own delight, "we'll have to get you changed into your Sunday best and we need to let the countess and Miss Hamilton get ready themselves."

Maeve had a simple plan for getting changed. Angus answered the door to let them in.

"Angus, have Kat draw two baths for us immediately, then attend to me in my bedroom. Have Mrs Morton come to the library straight away and come yourself with her."

"Yes, milady."

"Do you want me to stay?" Fi whispered as Angus walked away to seek out Mrs Morton.

"Yes, although we're very pressed for time with the games opening shortly."

"Let me see what I can do," she replied, slipping away in the other direction to Angus' departure, calling for the housekeeper as she went.

True to form, Angus reported to the library five minutes later, but empty-handed, explaining that he couldn't find Mrs Morton anywhere.

"That's alright, Angus," Maeve said, "tell me, did you think to look in the kitchens?"

"The kitchens, milady?" definitely sent back as a question.

"That's where I found her," Fi stepped from behind a set of bookshelves, beckoning for Mrs Morton to follow.

"Now, we've limited time, but I feel I have something that needs to be said." Maeve hadn't meant to waste valuable time lecturing these two old servants, but she had little option. It was make or break time with these two. There followed a hastily put-together, but passion-ridden appeal to them to cooperate for the greater good.

Angus blushed considerably, like a schoolboy, Maeve thought. Mrs Morton kept her eyes focused on her shoes, mumbling acquiescence when required.

"Now, to the point directly concerning me," Maeve said, moving the discussion on, "I need to know whether there are any dress conventions for me attending the Highland Games. I don't want to let the side down. I most specifically don't want to find out after the event that I've upset anyone through my ignorance, so please spill the beans now. Is that understood?"

Thirty minutes later, Fi opened the car door for the countess, noting the splendid sight she made.

"You look quite the treasure, Lady Strathfulton," she said as she admired the slender figure wrapped in tartan, with an elegant Robertson kilt topped by a splendid puffy blouse and a matching tartan ribbon tied around her neck. Her court shoes shone to perfection with her long legs in smart white socks ending in the same tartan on beribboned garters. As Fi looked up to eye level, she couldn't but help noticing the tartan beret perched on her carefully braided hair, yet more ribbons stretching down her back.

"Thank you, Fi. We're up against it on time, but I would still beg you not to drive too fast. I don't want to arrive white as a sheet and looking like I've just come through a gale!"

"Understood, Lady Strathfulton, and I shall act according to your wishes. Will you sit in the back?"

"No," Maeve answered, "I would prefer your company in the front." Maeve had a question to put to the remarkably fine young lady she had taken on as her secretary and had soon become the best of friends. She felt compelled to ask it and now was as good a time as any. "Besides," she added, "there's something I really want to ask you."

"Of course, Lady Strathfulton, I've been sort of expecting something with regards to my mother."

"There's a little more to it than meets the eye," Maeve replied, "but let's get underway and we can talk while you drive."

Chapter Thirteen

The presentation of gifts, indeed the whole opening ceremony for the games, went like a dream. Maeve felt herself central to the proceedings, with all eyes on her. As the owner of pretty well everything within view, that could be expected, heightened, of course, by the fact that she was a woman and a Sassenach or 'ootlin' as she heard herself referred to several times.

At first, she felt a fraud in her tartan; while she must have Scottish blood somewhere in her veins in order to inherit a brace of Scottish earldoms, she felt a complete outsider with Cardiff a long way from Fort William or Inverness, the only settlements of any size anywhere near the Strathfulton estate.

She was an object of interest such that all eyes were on her. And, with growing confidence, she felt like most of those pairs of eyes had a generally approving view as they regarded her.

. . .

Somehow Pudding had created an impressive set of presents, both attractive to look at, but also with a practical use. Thus, there were stones decorated beautifully with pictures of Highland life and transitioned into paperweights. There were also bookends made from horseshoes, thankfully positioned the correct way up for luck. The cream of the crop, however, was an exquisite wood carving of a golden eagle perched on a rocky crag, it's beady eyes presumably focused on prey in the meadows far below. This was intended for the Games Coordinator, an ancient looked specimen of a Highlander who seemed to talk without a mouth, such was the dense extent of his driven snow beard that wobbled with the cadence of his voice.

"I did start that some months ago," Pudding admitted, "thinking it might come in handy."

"So, you knew?"

"Well, when the old earl went sort of wild, Miss Countess, I thought who would carry on with the really important things? Not that he ever did any of the presents, but he would have someone do it for him because Mrs Morton would remind him each year and organise it on his behalf when he did nothing about it. But, this year, she seemed strangely preoccupied."

"So, you, my dear little thing, stepped up to the plate with your own ideas?"

"Well, I didn't want the tradition broken, so I rushed around preparing a few things. Then, when you arrived, I thought you must have it in hand and my presents wouldn't be needed. Then you told me of your problem yesterday and I thought 'yes, I can help after all'."

"Pudding to the rescue," Fi laughed, but, later on, Maeve heard her telling Pudding she had done an excellent job and that, "if you ever wanted a position as assistant to the assistant to the countess, you'll be first in the queue."

After the opening duties were done, they spent a pleasant few hours with Fi introducing Maeve to all the tenants in attendance, as well as to a variety of local residents. Fi, for a slip of a seventeen-year-old, seemed to know everyone. Most people warmed to her, not being able to hide the smile that she brought out of them, but a few turned their back, even though it meant turning their back on the new countess.

"I swear I shall never remember so many people's names," Maeve said half-way through the morning.

"That's what I felt when I went to boarding school," Fi replied while taking a pit stop in the light refreshment tent, "there were just swarms of girls all dressed the same. In fact, even the teachers all looked the same with their funny mortar boards. However, within half-a-term I knew everybody by name and could run on sight from the particularly pesky of the teachers who might give you detention because you'd let your socks slip down or were running in the corridor."

"You went to boarding school? I didn't know." There was actually a lot Maeve didn't know about Fi Hamilton. Mrs Hamilton, too, for that matter. As for the mysterious Mr

Hamilton, never mentioned by anyone, other than as being a busy man often away on sorting out his affairs.

"Well, yes," Fi reminisced, "I did actually, from the age of eleven to fourteen and then the…"

"Yes, Fi, and then what happened? Did the school burn down because the girls were smoking in the sports shed?" She had read a book about that on the train when first going from her native Cardiff to Oxfordshire to join the constabulary which had just opened up to female police officers. That had been a boys' school, but presumably girls got up to similar tricks, didn't they?

"No, it's funny you should say that but it was nothing so exciting, despite the rhyme we all sang as term came close to ending." Fi gathered her thoughts and then burst into song with the most delightful voice:

> *Build a bonfire, build a bonfire,*
> *Put the teachers on the top*
> *Put the prefects in the middle*
> *And burn the bloody lot.*

"And there's another one – how did it go then?"

After a hushed moment, she broke out again:

> *Ten more days to go*
> *Ten more days of sorrow*
> *Ten more days in this old dump*
> *And we'll be home tomorrow.*

Death in a Classroom

No more Latin, no more French
No more sitting on the old school bench

The last two lines were delivered with a delightful chant, almost as if Maeve could hear and imagine the girls counting down the days to the holidays and freedom. Maeve had heard stories of boarding school from Freddie Blythe, also in line for a Scottish earldom, but seldom resident in Scotland because of his deep friendship with Cess Pitt who lived with her mother, Mrs Robinson, at Darriby Hall.

Maeve had been happy to be based as the sergeant at Darriby. But now she shook herself, aware that this was a new life she was facing, one that fate had sent her way; it was incumbent upon her to make the most of it.

"So, what did happen to your boarding school career, Fi?" Maeve asked as the burst of song appeared to be spent.

"Oh, well, the truth is, um…"

"You can tell me, my dear. We're friends are we not?"

"Well, you see Daddy couldn't afford it anymore so I came back home and…"

"And haven't been to school since?"

"Yes, but I'm too old for that stuff now, don't you think, Maeve?"

"I suppose you do just have to make your own way in the world now. I can't see you going back to school, Fi. Besides, why do you need to? You've got a great live-in job helping me."

The truth was, Maeve had come to rely on Fi enormously, and this was only her third day of employment.

Everyone who was anyone, and a lot more of those that weren't, came to the Highland games. Maeve, as the hottest new aristocrat in the whole of Scotland, was passed from one honourable to another, whisked to meet Lord MacSomebody, then whisked again to stand before another with a remarkably similar name. Most had beards and heavy moustaches; Maeve imagined these to be insulation against the cold, having heard lots of comments about fair weather invaders from south of the border. Unfortunately, they had fixed in her mind that she was English and no amount of concentration on the difference between England and Wales seemed to make the slightest bit of difference.

She was a Sassenach, and that was about the end of it, although she much preferred the term 'ootlin' and even tried bringing it into conversations as her confidence grew, trying to create awareness that there were people of similar origin on the fringes of the British Isles. Most of the people she met soon slipped back to 'you English, if you don't mind me saying so, are always... doing this or doing that.'

This peeved her a little, but it was one of those things. They didn't seem to recognise that there was Celtic stock outside Hibernia.

Still, it was fun to slowly decipher their accents sufficiently to ask them about their families, trying to recall which ones she had asked already, muttering their names under her breath in an attempt to remember them for next time.

This was her world now and she needed to make the most of it.

Then, in the crowd she saw a figure she didn't particularly want to see. It had been puzzling her as to how she could ever get on with Mrs Morton. And now the woman was striding towards her from across the other side of the field.

She was an older woman, but one for whom unfulfilled purpose came out in the way she walked.

And, despite her servant status, one who seemed to carve a route through the crowd, with people naturally stepping back to get out of her way.

"Ah there you are, Lady Strathfulton," came a voice from behind her. She turned, almost knocking the speaker down.

"Mrs Hamilton, how nice to see you." This could be a double opportunity, the chance to avoid Mrs Morton, if she could manage it so, and a way to find out more about the Hamilton family as well.

"How is Fi doing?" Mrs Hamilton asked, "do you want to send her back yet?" Maeve couldn't work out whether that was said from spite or as a joke. She rather hoped the latter as she did not want to think ill of her new friend's mother.

Although, she was suspect number one on her list of possible murderers of poor Mr MacGregor, with whom Fi had been, she strongly suspected, about to elope.

Her list of suspects that actually started and ended with Mrs Hamilton.

. . .

"Well, I'll tell you all about the little dear," Maeve replied, "but I'm parched and would relish a visit to the only tent I haven't been into yet."

"I'll lead the way, shall I, Lady Strathfulton?" Another strider; it seemed the Highlands grew their women to stretch out their legs and leave the poor 'ootlins' far behind.

Armed with a large whisky apiece, for which Maeve was developing a taste, she gave a fun verbal dissertation on the wonders of Fi Hamilton, secretary extraordinaire, including her amusing tendency to always be in the garden, noting how Mrs Hamilton's pride made her stand tall, even though they were sitting at an old wood table that rocked precariously with the slightest weight upon it.

Maeve then tried to move the subject onto the older generation of Hamiltons.

"Tell me, Mrs Hamilton, something of the Hamilton history in Strathfulton, if you don't mind, that is."

"We're as old as the bens," she said with a brittle laugh that made Maeve determined to find out more, despite the fact that Mrs Hamilton seemed equally determined to skirt around this particular ben, rather than climb up the side of it.

"Why didn't you approve of Mr MacGregor?" Maeve didn't know where that question came from. She drained her Scotch and indicated to the waiter for replenishment.

"Why don't you try the Strathfulton single malt?" Mrs Hamilton said, making Maeve think it an attempt to avoid the question she hadn't even meant to ask.

"Yes, that would be nice, seeing as I own the distillery."

Then, Mrs Hamilton surprised her by answering the question she hadn't meant to ask. She did it directly and fully.

"I did disapprove of Mr MacGregor because I felt him to be a bad influence on Fi. Everyone saw him as a saint, working diligently at the school, but I knew about his other activities because..." And then she stopped, rose from her seat and left the hospitality tent without looking back or saying goodbye. She even left behind an untouched glass of Strathfulton single malt.

Because what? Maeve was left wondering, swirling her Scotch around her glass, deep in thought, her eyes taking in the beautiful shades of her drink as it formed mini-waves inside her glass; was it a storm in the brewing? There was clearly a lot more to this death in a classroom than first met the eye. And how did Mr Hamilton's 'business trips' fit with whatever explanation she was being denied for some reason she just could not grasp.

She disapproved of Mr MacGregor because of what? Perhaps knowing that would be the first step to solving the mystery.

But, with neither Hamilton prepared to talk, how on earth could she ever hope to find out?

Chapter Fourteen

*T*ime stands still for no man, no woman either, whatever her exalted rank. Thus, this splendid, yet exasperating, day wound on towards evening. Maeve made several more trips to the hospitality tent, including a lunch, if not quite fit for a prince, at least perfectly good fare for a countess. In between, she judged this and judged that, everything from dogs to cabbages, rabbits to pottery and poetry; this whole process involved shaking a lot of hands and finding suitable things to say to total strangers.

Something, she realised, she was above average at doing. In fact, as her confidence grew, she even considered herself rather good at it.

Throughout this varied day, Maeve kept a sharp lookout for two people: Mrs Hamilton, who she was desperate to meet again, in order to continue the gentle lines of enquiry she had started over the quite delicious Strathfulton single malt, of which she was delighted to be the owner, and Mrs Morton, who she was equally determined to avoid.

She failed on both counts. Mrs Hamilton was nowhere to be seen, while Mrs Morton came bounding up to the motor car just before Maeve climbed in to return to the castle. Fi was staying behind to ensure preparations were ready for the second and final day of the games.

"Ah, there you are, milady, would you be kind enough to offer me a lift back to the castle? I'm afraid my body's not quite what it was these days and I have to admit to a little exhaustion." Maeve suspected another reason why Mrs Morton sought her company; she had, after all, been searching for her earlier. But, she recognised she had little choice in the matter.

"Certainly, Mrs Morton, the more the merrier. No, Fi won't be driving, I will, while you ride sidecar and pepper the bad fellows with the machine gun."

When she got no response to this, she tried restating her joke, explaining it in different words, then abandoned that approach when she realised that Mrs Morton had no sense of humour.

Not only did she lack it now, but she probably never had had a sense of humour, nor ever would develop one.

"You can come in the front with me," she said bluntly.

"Are you sure, milady?" Something told Maeve that this had been the woman's intention all along; for some reason, she wanted ten minutes alone with her new employer. Whatever that reason, Maeve would find out soon enough. She had to remember that information was welcome because she was otherwise in total darkness, about her role on the estate she now owned.

And of course, about the murder that had occurred on the day of her arrival at Strathfulton.

She did find out, for Mrs Morton started talking the moment the car rolled out of its reserved parking spot and made for the exit gate.

"Milady, I wanted to start with a sincere apology for entirely forgetting to inform you about the presents for the organisers of the games."

Maeve heard the words but judged it best not to respond, not yet at any rate; let Mrs Morton play out enough rope to hang herself with. Maeve had the plausible enough excuse of concentrating on the impossibly narrow lanes which wound around all over the place.

"What, with you arriving so suddenly," Mrs Morton continued, "and with Mr Macgregor being found dead at his desk, it's a wonder I have any wits about me at all!" Ah, so the woman did have a sense of humour, at least when it suited her. It's just, Maeve considered, that it's totally subservient to whatever higher cause Mrs Morton followed.

Which she now laid out in what Maeve thought to be a deliberately hesitant and artificial manner.

"Milady," she began the moment Maeve pulled onto a reasonably level and straight stretch of road, "there has... been something... something, well, bothering me about bringing... Miss Hamilton into the castle. I've, eh, um, thought long and hard about whether to speak up and finally decided that my duty to you, as Countess of

Strathfulton and Baritone, dictates that I say something, however unpleasant it may sound to foreign ears." Was that a reference to the fact that Maeve was a citizen of distant Wales, coming to Scotland for the first time just days ago?

"And what might that be?" she turned to look at Mrs Morton sitting next to her in the front of the car, then had to look back at the road as she handled a sharp bend badly and swung the car out towards a pony on a hack. "I'm sorry," she called after sliding open the window, battling to get the vehicle under control.

"That's alright, Miss Countess," came a voice she knew so well.

"Pudding, it's you. You have a horse?"

"Yes, Mamma has a big one too. We often ride together."

"I shall watch out on the bends more carefully in future, Pudding."

Mrs Morton's contribution to this conversation was to announce, once Maeve had driven on, that Pudding was a nice girl from nice stock.

"But that's not what you wanted to talk to me about, is it now, Mrs Morton?"

"No, milady, it was more about the bad influence of the Hamilton family. You do know, for instance, that Mr Hamilton is not exactly a model of honesty?" Ah, so it would come out this way, Maeve thought; she would get the truth of the matter, just not from Mrs Hamilton or Fi.

That, she supposed, was sensible given the intense

embarrassment that must sit on the shoulders of the Hamilton family.

But it only made sense if she could rely on a true interpretation from her housekeeper.

"Go on," she said, but eyes firmly on the road after her near miss with Pudding and pony.

"Well," Mrs Morton replied, "you know that Mr Hamilton is 'away on business', milady?"

"Yes, Mrs Hamilton said as much."

"Well, it's a certain type of business, milady, one involving His Majesty, if you get my meaning, milady."

In reply, Maeve, instinctively put on a bored voice, telling her passenger that she knew that very well indeed, but stopping short of informing Mrs Morton that she had worked it out rather than being informed of the circumstances.

"Ah, so you knew... milady?" Maeve heard these words with regret. Had she silenced Mrs Morton too early with her claim to know everything? Should she have played the ignorant bystander a bit longer?

"Yes," Maeve replied after a moment of deep thought, disguised as concentration on the road, "but being a former sergeant in the police, I have an inherent love of getting every angle on a story, so I would be very pleased to hear what you have to say, Mrs Morton." She congratulated herself on turning the situation around; one glance Mrs Morton's way told her she had done so.

"Very well, milady, I shall tell you exactly as it is, if you're ready, milady?"

Maeve nodded to indicate her state of readiness and then relaxed as she turned onto the main road for the short distance to Strathfulton Castle. She had put the winding lanes behind her.

It happened like this. Mr Hamilton came from good stock, so I can't imagine what turned him the way it did. Other than, perhaps, the thought of embarrassment at reducing his inherited wealth down to pauper status in just ten or a dozen years. At one point, the Hamilton family had been dominant in these parts, then the Strathfultons rose and the Hamiltons declined in equal measure, that being a process that went on over generation after generation and really concluded some years ago.

By the time we get to the outbreak of war, and the death of old Major Hamilton in the first few days of August 1914, our Mr Hamilton thus inheriting, the family fortune was down to a few farms scatted amongst the Strathfulton holdings. I must add that the Strathfultons lacked, at this time, able leadership, the earldom being in the hands of the old earl, then a mere teenager, but due for an unhappy meeting with death, dangling at the end of a rope, that being just last year. I'm sorry, milady, I'll keep to the point. Yes, now, where was I?

Yes, that's it. Mr Hamilton concocted a wicked plan to swindle the Earl of Strathfulton out of several valuable landholdings just a few years ago, wanting to restore, in some small measure, the fortunes of the Hamilton clan. Apparently, he drew up some land transfer documents and a certain schoolteacher by the name of

Mr MacGregor forged the earl's signature on the documents. I don't know what Mr MacGregor's motivation for this act was, no doubt pecuniary in some manner or other. He is, or was, a person much motivated by money.

"Mrs Morton, this is a most extraordinary tale. How do you know it's true?" Maeve had stopped the car in the middle of the road. She turned to look at the narrator, both hands clamping the steering wheel as if, without her grip it would fall to the floor of the vehicle.

Trying hard to clamp a grip onto this strange new world too.

Ah, I see you're ready for chapter two, milady! Their plan almost worked, based, as it was, on the eccentricity of the old earl. In this matter, Mr Hamilton was exceedingly clever. You see, it was a conceivable action on his part to sell off lands his father had originally purchased from the Hamiltons. You must understand, milady, that they were not part of the entail which, as you know, can only be passed to the next relative. Hence, in dire need of money, it was perfectly possible that he sold off what he could; indeed, he did similar with several artworks and, I'm to understand, all his stocks and shares too.

It failed, as do so many such brilliant plans, on a minor detail, combined, you'll be pleased to hear, milady, with the eagle-eyed nature of a young police officer at the time. This particular officer was charged with going over the case file one final time, prior to it being filed away in the archives as an unresolved case. The officer checked a few dates of key events, well aware that they had been checked and checked again. He looked at the date on the contracts of sale and something didn't quite feel right. Flicking through the rest of the folder, he found what he was looking for and took it straight to his boss.

The day the old earl had apparently signed the contractual land transfers, he was actually on remand in some prison down in England of all places. How could he have signed those contracts when inside at His Majesty' pleasure?

The arrests happened very quickly. Thankfully, for all those involved, the trial was held in Edinburgh, away from the local gaze. Mr Hamilton was found guilty and sentenced to three years in prison.

By that time, of course, the old earl had made his escape from custody and was causing havoc all over England. Hence, the press concentrated on the earl and Mr Hamilton's fate went largely unnoticed.

"I see," Maeve realised she had the vehicle standing in the middle of the main road, blocking the route for any other traffic. "But, I don't understand how this sad story led to the death of Mr MacGregor." She slipped the car into gear and released the clutch so it rumbled forward, shaking as it picked up speed.

"Oh, that must be obvious, milady," Mrs Morton replied as they turned into the drive and rattled past the gatehouse where Pudding lived with her mother. "Mr Hamilton was jailed, but Mr MacGregor hired a fancy lawyer and got off scot free. My belief is that Mr Hamilton organised the murder from his own jail cell."

"The motive?"

"Vengeance, milady, pure unadulterated vengeance. There's not much good in that family, that's something I can say for certain, even if other things are as clear as mud!"

Chapter Fifteen

It was food for thought. But, a little more thought told her that there still had to be a man on the ground, the one who thrust the knife up under the ribs to break violently into Mr MacGregor's heart.

Man on the ground? Or person on the ground? Could it have been Mrs Hamilton who made short work of the schoolteacher? Mrs Hamilton had reason to hate Mr MacGregor twice over. First, he had been, according to Fi, about to elope with her daughter, the ultimate, perhaps, in disgrace for an already disgraced family. Second, she probably blamed Mr MacGregor for her husband being sent away on His Majesty's Pleasure.

There was another question to consider. Fi was no fool. If Mrs Morton knew the facts, so did Fi. So, why hadn't Fi told her? It was time, she considered, to ask Fi a direct question or two. She would do that as soon as she caught up with her.

. . .

She got her chance an hour or so later when Fi returned. Maeve had dressed for supper already, aided by Kat, and caught Fi as she went up to change.

"Fi, there's something I would ask you." She had run it through her mind a hundred times, different variations of the same question.

"Can it wait, Maeve? No?"

"I'll follow you up to your room. Where is it, by the way?"

"Top floor, so I hope you're not too exhausted from walking the field all day long."

Maeve tried to ask her question, surprised and distracted that Fi led the way to one of the back stairs.

"Fi, did you... well, this isn't easy to ask, but... so I'll come straight out with it." Think yourself as Sergeant Morgan, she said to herself, questions must be put and they must also be answered. "Um, yes, did you gain from the death of Mr MacGregor?"

"No, Maeve."

"Will you gain?"

"Only from his life assurance and his stocks and shares."

Blow, Maeve thought, as she followed Fi up a third flight of stairs, narrower than any she had been on in her few days as owner of Strathfulton Castle.

"How much?"

"Um," now, it seemed, it was Fi's turn to hesitate in awkwardness.

"Maybe a few thousand?"

"A bit more, Maeve."

"Five?"

"Up a bit." They went on, the figure climbing as they climbed physically up staircase after staircase.

"It can't be thirty-thousand?"

"That's what the lawyer said. Half stocks and shares and then there's the life assurance, made out to me, his fiancé."

"Gosh, Fi, that's a lot of money."

"Yes, and I know exactly what I'm going to do with it. You see, money bores me, but what it can do for others really interests me."

Maeve stepped back to look at her friend cum secretary and part-time gardener. Suddenly, she realised that they were right up at the top of the house, in the attics somewhere.

"You can't live up here?" she said, "it must be a mistake."

"No, this is where Mrs Morton put me."

"I'll have you moved straight away," Maeve replied, blushing in indignation.

"I rather like my room," Fi replied, "besides, I'd miss Kat if I moved out."

"You share with Kat?" Maeve couldn't understand this. Fi was a senior figure in the household, yet was being treated by Mrs Morton as the most junior. The castle was said to have a hundred bedrooms, yet Mrs Morton had put Fi to share one in the servants' quarters.

"She'll be putting you in a uniform next," Maeve commented, rather liking her own joke.

"Well, she's ordered them, just like Kat's so we'll be sisters together, that's what she said, at any rate. I've never had a sister." Fi's reply astonished Maeve, coming from somewhere completely off the pitch.

"Let me think on this," Maeve replied eventually, "anyway, I've asked my question so I'll leave you to get changed. I'll see you in the drawing room."

Maeve later heard that Fi was spot on timewise, despite her late arrival back from the games. Maeve, however, was twenty-minutes late, having spent half-an-hour getting completely lost in the biggest house, she was sure, in the world.

A far cry from the neat little semi-detached, brand new and fit-for-heroes, that she had grown up on in a leafy street on the outskirts of Cardiff.

Supper was a satisfyingly quiet affair. Apparently, Friday evening was Mrs Morton's night off so Kat served both Maeve and Fi under the overall direction of a slightly inebriated Angus who compensated for too much enjoyment in the Strathfulton Games hospitality tent by appearing overly solemn as he plodded around the room with Kat doing all the finer aspects of serving. Kat was a little bit silly with her roommate, Fi, but Maeve put it down to youthful high spirits and thought no more of it; she wanted to concentrate on what she had heard that day; first, a hint from Mrs Hamilton, then a diatribe against the Hamiltons from Mrs Morton, finally the revelation from Fi of a substantial inheritance from her fiancé, Mr MacGregor, combined with an evident disinterest in worldly matters.

It all amounted to a puzzle she couldn't get her mind around.

"I think I shall take a walk in the garden," Maeve said when supper was finished. "What will you do, Fi?"

"Oh, do you mind, because it's Mrs Morton's day off, if I have some time with Kat?" Maeve agreed; she couldn't really deny this remarkable girl a bit of fun. A part of her wanted to draw a line between served and server, but another part cried out that life is too short to live by rules every moment of every day.

Thus, Maeve let Fi go up to their tiny bedroom and chat and have fun with Kat, while she went off alone to walk amongst the gardens that wrapped around the castle in every direction, mostly overgrown as the two remaining gardeners were far too old to do useful work, and certainly couldn't manage forty acres.

But, not alone for long, because her feet followed a pattern without her knowledge, and that pattern took her along the side of the drive, through the squat beech tree wood and down towards the gate.

Not to Pudding, sent to bed an hour or so earlier, but to the entrance to the cottage they lived in, the old gatehouse, and to Mrs Reid, Pudding's mother, in the low-ceilinged kitchen.

"Hello, Lady Strathfulton," she said, straightening up from the oven, "the rolls are almost ready, so I'll put the kettle on."

"Thank you, Mrs Reid, the walk has given me quite a thirst so a cup of tea would be most welcome."

A few minutes later, Maeve sat across the kitchen table from Mrs Reid, a large, brim-full cup in front of her and a roll with butter from the home farm and Mrs Reid's homemade jam to her left.

"This is delicious," she said, taking a bite, "my goodness, how delectable bread and jam can be!"

"The simple things," Mrs Reid said, "are often the best. But, you have something on your mind, do you not, Lady Strathfulton?"

"I do, several things, in fact." Maeve told her much of what she had heard that day.

"I'd just warn ye to be careful," Mrs Reid said after listening to a recounting of Mrs Morton's words that day. "Mr Hamilton is a fine gentleman who took a wrong turning in life and is paying a high price. There is even some talk about whether he is really guilty at all."

"How could I find out more about the case?"

"Well, it would be a bit much to go all the way to Edinburgh," Mrs Reid said, explaining that she had never been and didn't care to go either. "I know Barry liked it," she added pensively.

"Barry?" Her predecessor, the earl, had been Barry Baritone.

"Oh, it's nothing," Mrs Reid replied, "I say Barry just to say a name. No, Lady Strathfulton, I can't lie. I too have a story to tell."

"I'd love to hear it," Maeve said, thinking when you have insoluble mysteries, why not add another mystery in a layer over that? There was a pudding the cook at Darriby Hall had made with layers of pastry over fruit fillings tinged with sugar. Quite delicious, so why not make a Mystery Pudding of all the mysteries about this strange, but growing-on-one, place?

"Well, Lady Strathfulton, may I suggest something a bit stronger than a cup of tea?" She went to the cupboard in the kitchen and pulled out a bottle of Strathfulton 15-year single malt.

"I'm all ears," Maeve said as she sipped the delightful whisky she was responsible for, recalling that this was three 'wee drams' today alone; she was getting a taste for it.

"If you're ready, then I'll begin, but hush child so I can tell the tale." Maeve looked around and saw that she was the only person in the kitchen other than Mrs Reid. Hence, she deduced that she had been relegated to the status of a child.

The story, when it eventually came, turned Maeve's mind in somersaults.

"I've no idea of the relationship," she said when Mrs Reid finally finished, "but there is one, of that much I'm sure."

Chapter Sixteen

"You mean Pudding is...?" Maeve couldn't get her mind around it.

"You've got to bear in mind that the old earl started alright but something blew him right off the rails," Mrs Reid replied, "I mean he completely lost it at the end, the poor man." She said that with sufficient sorrow for Maeve to look up from her whisky glass and straight into the eyes of her companion, the single mother of Lilias Reid, also known as Pudding. She saw depths to the woman she never would have imagined, knowing instantly that, as long as she lived at Strathfulton Castle, Mrs Reid, just like her daughter, would be someone she could lean on.

"You had strong feelings for Barry?" she said, thinking back to the endless scandals he had caused in Oxfordshire. She had seen him as a nasty piece of work, but here was another perspective emerging.

"We were very much in love, but her mother, the dowager countess, wouldn't entertain the thought of marriage to the daughter of a tenant farmer, albeit it a highly respectable one. When he told his mother I was with child, she threw a fit and sent Barry to England, banishing him from ever coming to Strathfulton again. She moved to Baritone Abbey and I was given this cottage and a pension, not, I might add, with particularly good grace."

"My dear," Maeve said, "what a terrible thing to do."

"There's more," Mrs Reid replied, "you see I was born a Morrison."

"I've seen that name in the estate records. The Morrisons over in..."

"Brackinton, Lady Strathfulton, where we've been for generations."

And, Maeve thought, she remembered the name. They had stood out in the estate records as being one of the few tenants who were paid up with their rent, never a question of falling into arrears.

"But, I don't understand, your surname."

"That was Lady Strathfulton's doing as well, the dowager Lady Strathfulton, I mean, not you, of course."

"No, I know, Mrs Reid. Did the dowager countess arrange a husband for you?"

"Yes, a brute of a man called John Reid. Uncouth and prone to violence, he ruled this house with terror for the first seven years of poor Lilias' life before very conveniently dying of a massive heart attack at the age of forty-two. I didn't shed a single tear when that man died, although he left me with debts aplenty."

Maeve knew Mrs Reid had shed many tears in her thirty-odd years on this earth, just none for John Reid. Now that she had heard the story, she could see the sadness just below the pretty features of her host, where she sat at the kitchen table as if she were any other visitor apart from the countess.

"You know what this means, Mrs Reid," she said after a moment's quiet reflection, "I never fully grasped the relationship between Barry Baritone and myself, such that I inherited the land and the titles, but it means we're sort of related."

"Ah, I can tell you exactly the relationship, just a mo., Lady Strathfulton." She disappeared out of the kitchen and came back two minutes later with a large leather tube, suitable for housing a telescope, from which she drew out a roll of paper.

They used the bottle and glasses to hold the edges down after Mrs Reid stretched the parchment out on the table top.

"You'll be cousins," she said, "it's just a matter of degree."

"You're interested in genealogy?"

"Everything to do with history and the past intrigues me, Lady Strathfulton."

"Maeve."

"I'm sorry?"

"Call me Maeve, at least when we're on our own." Her words echoed those she had said to Fi just a few days ago. She might have arrived in a rainstorm, but friendship had shone down on her ever since she had pulled in at Strathfulton station. She felt a surge of warmth strike through her, exactly as one does on the first warm day of the year.

"Well, I'm Lilias, just like my daughter. Barry, well, he wrote me letters whenever he could, I mean before the illness took hold of him and he headed so badly downhill. So, I know that he wanted the next generation to be a reminder of me, so to speak. But, I've always been known as Lily, whereas Lilias has become Pudding."

"Lily, such a lovely name."

"Thank you... Maeve."

After smiling in recognition of the new connection between them, they went back to the Strathfulton and Baritone family tree, to find the other connection.

"It seems you're related to poor Barry twice over. Once through your father and once through your mother. Both times it is..." she bent over the table again, following the lines up to a common point. "Yes, both times it's second cousins."

"What does that make Pudding to me?"

"Second cousin once removed."

"Will you tell her?"

"Not until she's older. She might find it quite a shock."

They chatted quite a lot longer, mainly with Lily giving the background to Strathfulton that Maeve so desperately wanted. No, she needed it, not only to understand all the quirks and peculiarities of a great landed estate, but also if she had any chance of discovering who had murdered poor Mr MacGregor.

That is, poor if he deserved the title and didn't prove to be the villain some people thought he was.

"Why is Pudding still at primary school?" Maeve asked at one point.

"Because she's such a strange mixture. I often think she gets steadiness from me and the wildness from her father. She's useless at reading and writing, but so practical and down-to-earth."

"Lily, would you be willing to send her to the castle once a week, say on a Saturday morning so it doesn't disrupt with school?"

"What for, Maeve? You mean for remedial lessons? Yes, I'd love to have her do those with you, but we'll have a job catching her."

"Who is going to teach the children when they go back on Monday?" Maeve asked.

"Ah, I heard it was to be a committee of volunteers on a rota basis, because of the pending closure."

"The closure? I know nothing about that. Why on earth is the school closing? It seemed jam-packed in there."

"Didn't Mrs Morton tell you?"

"Lily, something you have to know about Mrs Morton. She specialises in telling me nothing. But, I shall ask her first thing in the morning. Now, I must be going, or morning shall be upon us and neither would have gotten a wink of sleep, isn't that the case? Goodnight, Lily, it's been splendid talking to you. I'm so glad I came."

"Well, I'm glad you came too, Maeve, so goodnight and sweet dreams, at least for what is left of the night."

The next morning brought a promise of sunshine, the type where the heat creeps up on one during the day. A tinge of frost or fog in the morning would quickly burn off, replaced with a brilliant blue sky and steadily increasing temperatures, such that whatever clothes one started the day with would be hopelessly unsuitable come the afternoon.

Kat brought Maeve her tea at exactly six o'clock, bobbing her way into Maeve's bedroom and opening the curtains to the sunshine that dared to penetrate the light fog at that early hour.

"Good morning, Kat," she said, rubbing the sleep from her eyes.

"Good morning, milady. Did you know someone came looking for you last night?"

"Who was that?" She had let herself into the sleeping castle a little after midnight after walking back from the gatehouse. She was pleased that nobody had waited up for her, but that had meant she only now learned about the visitor.

"It was a Mr Munro, milady." Kat was a sweet girl, bobbing every time she spoke, like an apple in a tub of water. "He said he would come back for you this morning, milady."

"Oh, I thought he had gone back to Inverness." That was interesting news. Robert Munro was handsome and charming, clever too. She rather liked the idea of him coming back in the morning.

That led to a huge decision on what to wear. Surprisingly, timid young Kat took charge, saying a summer dress would do fine, especially for the games running their second and final day.

"I don't think, milady, a jacket and skirt quite as much fun as that lovely summer dress, milady." That sentence actually consisted of three distinct curtseys, perhaps Kat was a little nervous about disagreeing with her mistress.

"Then dress it shall be, Kat, thank you so much for helping me select it. I shall appoint you my fashion consultant."

"Thank you, milady, you see, I do love clothes. Not the type I wear when not on duty, but the lovely ones you have."

Maeve couldn't agree more. She had spent a considerable amount of the available cash on a new wardrobe while staying at her London home before getting the sleeper train to Scotland.

"Tell me, Kat, did you go to the school in the village?"

"For a few years, milady, until Mamma got sick and needed me at home. Then when she got better, it didn't seem that important."

"How did you find Mr MacGregor?"

"Oh, that's the thing, milady. I know Fi, I mean, Miss Hamilton, had a thing for him, but I never liked him that much."

Maeve desperately wanted to ask about the Hamiltons, particularly Mr MacGregor's role in his 'going away' for three years, but she couldn't ask this girl, who was little more than a child.

More and more, she felt the true character of Mr MacGregor was vital to understanding who was responsible for his murder. Sad to say, being from the police herself, she had little to zero confidence in Cyril Clarke and DI Cassidy. Cliché Clarke seemed more interested in fishing than solving a murder, while Cassidy wanted the bottle more than justice and law and order. She had seen him, yesterday, in the hospitality tent, no doubt drinking his overnight allowance all over again.

Going back to the true character, Mr MacGregor had been marked down by Mrs Hamilton and, most definitely, by Mrs Morton, yet Fi had been most determinedly in love with him.

Who was right?

Why did it seem so important?

And what was this about the school closure?

There were mysteries everywhere she turned.

At least one thing was clear. Robert Munro liked Maeve. He made that obvious with the huge bunch of flowers he brought when he came back at 7am, while Maeve was still at breakfast. A breakfast at which Mrs Morton was strangely absent, with Kat and Fi handling the kippers and scrambled egg in her place, and doing a remarkably good job of it, although not being terribly quiet in the process.

"Kat, would you mind putting these in water and putting the jug in my bedroom? And, then please scour the whole castle for Mrs Morton, if you'd be so kind. Mr Munro, you must have some kippers."

"Well, I am rather partial to kippers," he replied with that boyish grin that made him look eighteen instead of early thirties. "Lady Strathfulton, would you do me the honour of allowing me to escort you to the games this morning?"

"That would be delightful, Mr Munro," she replied, "we could stock up on breakfast and then go straight along there, could we not?"

Mrs Morton was found and not very far from the first place that Angus said he had looked. Kat bumped into her going up the stairs to look for her in the rooms she had on the top floor, but with a different staircase to the main servants' quarters. The ground floor of the castle was hard enough for Maeve to find her way around, but the upper floors were a myriad of confusing steps and stairs with winding passageways in between, reminding Maeve of Fi's words about her first days at boarding school.

A minute or two later, Mrs Morton was explaining herself to her employer, with her employer's legal representative in attendance, plus the most junior member of staff who had managed to retreat to a corner of the vast library without being noticed.

"I'm sorry, milady, you see it's Mr Morton. He's not too well, you see and I had, um, yes, you see, I had to rush home. He won't be at the games, now, not even for his beloved hammer throw which he was champion at every year bar the war years."

"Is he alright now, Mrs Morton? Shall we call for the doctor?"

"No, milady, it doesn't warrant that. All I know is he needs rest in a dark room, milady. He's had these turns before."

"If you're sure, Mrs Morton?"

"I'm sure," she snapped, then adding a 'milady' in case it be interpreted as insolence.

"Right," said Robert Munro, "if that settles everything, I think we can head off to the field now. I don't want to miss the first few games. I do love the competitive spirit these games engender."

Chapter Seventeen

"I do believe that's your housekeeper trotting down the drive," Robert said as he and Maeve shared the backseat and Fi acted as chauffeur.

"Fi, better stop the car, in case she wants a lift to the games."

She didn't want a lift, in fact she looked very flustered as she panted out the next revelation.

"Mi... mi... milady," she gasped, "I... I did tell you, did... did I not?"

"Calm down Mrs Morton," Maeve said, "take a few deep breaths and think about what you're going to say." Maeve wondered whether she came across as patronising but didn't concern herself too much, as something nagged at her. There was something she had to ask Mrs Morton, something of importance that danced just beyond her memory.

"I'm sure I did say about the lunch today at the castle." Mrs Morton seemed to have regained some control.

"What lunch?"

"Why, the lunch to mark the closing of the games, milady, what else would it be?"

Maeve felt a blade of anger; the woman was verging on insolence again. She couldn't let this pass.

But someone else was there before she could summon the words.

"Mrs Morton," Robert said, coming around the back of the car to stand before her, "I hardly think that appropriate language for your employer and mistress."

"I was just saying... sir..." her voice petered out as another mood seemed to take her in hand. She curtseyed to the pair of them, then turned abruptly, as if on parade, and marched back up the drive.

"Wait!" Robert Munro called after her, but to no effect.

"It's alright, sir," Fi said, "I know what she's talking about. On closing the games, there's always a big lunch here at the castle. I expect Mrs Morton has invited the usual crowd but not remembered to tell you about it. She certainly seems to have a lot on her mind at present."

"Might I make a suggestion?" Robert said, going on to explain that Fi could drop them at the games and then return to the castle to liaise with Mrs Morton and Angus about the lunch.

"Yes, Robert, what a good idea. Fi, be sure to let them know that there are two extra for lunch. Robert, I hope you can make it?"

"Yes, I'd love to, thank you very much indeed. But, who is the other extra?"

"Fi, of course."

"Mrs Morton won't like that, Lady Strathfulton. She sees me as a servant rather than a friend of the family."

"Nevertheless, I want you there and it's my wishes that count in the matter."

They got back in the car but Maeve felt haunted by Mrs Morton because there was something she needed to ask the housekeeper but it kept escaping her. Back in the old days, in the force, everything was written down, hence follow up questions were easy. Perhaps she should resort to the same procedure if she had any hope of sorting out this dreadful murder?

Chapter Eighteen

As Maeve, Countess of Strathfulton and Baritone, entered her castle, she felt as if half the Highland games visitors had decamped to her home. There were people everywhere milling around, tweed suits seemed to prevail, whether housing formidable men or formidable ladies, that seemed to be the dress for the day.

Maeve felt somewhat left out in the summer dress that Kat had chosen. For half-a-second she wondered whether Kat had deliberately put her in a dress. After all, she didn't know Kat that well. Could it be a cruel joke?

Then she spotted her balancing a laden drinks tray in one hand, the other trying to make a way through the crowd of people. Whatever mischief may or may not be going on in Strathfulton, castle, estate or village, Kat was not a part of it.

Of that she could be certain.

But what was that mischief that left one man dead, murdered in his own classroom?

"Lady Strathfulton, how nice to see you again." She turned to see Mrs Hamilton, noting how the crowd parted like the Red Sea to let her through.

"Mrs Hamilton, could I see you for a moment? Privately?"

Mrs Hamilton nodded towards a door off the hall that Maeve had never used before. Indeed, she didn't remember even seeing it. She followed the older woman as if she were the visitor summoned to the castle that belonged to Mrs Hamilton.

The door opened. Mrs Hamilton slipped inside, Maeve following her. Suddenly, Maeve remembered that Mrs Hamilton remained the main suspect, although she increasingly doubted it; was it wise to disappear from sight with suspect number one?

The door led to a long passage with a flag-stoned floor and wooden panelling to chest height. Along the passage were alcoves set into the wall, each one containing a painting of Strathfulton scenery by the same artist, marked for their position and then 'Strathfulton' scribbled in the corner, if one can scribble with a paint brush.

"The old earl did these," Mrs Hamilton said, noting Maeve's appreciation of the paintings, "the last earl, I mean, for he wasn't that old at all."

"He had talent," Maeve replied, still a part of her wondering where she was being taken, for there were no doors to the passage.

Not, at least, until they got to the very end where a leaded light window shone glorious strands of red and green colour across the passage. There, to the right, was a tiny door down a half dozen steps.

"I thought you wouldn't know about this place," Mrs Hamilton said, leaning into the room beyond to hold the door open for Maeve.

For a matching half-second to the one where she had thought ill of Kat, Maeve now worried about Mrs Hamilton. Was this her style? To lure her away into some forgotten part of the castle and do away with her, hoping her remains would be skeletal by the time some workman stumbled upon her years later?

Her brain was let loose for that half-second, then her instinct returned to square things up. She knew Mrs Hamilton had no ill intentions.

Who, then, did? That was the question that burnt a hole in her curiosity.

"I believe, Lady Strathfulton, that I owe you an apology and an explanation. You see, Fi drove around to see me today after dropping you at the games. We ended up having quite a heart-to-heart about everything and I see things from a clearer perspective now."

"And?"

"And, hence, the apology followed by the explanation, or would you prefer the explanation and then the apology?"

She was smiling as she spoke and Maeve saw the same traits as with Fi. Neither were classically beautiful, but they had a way of making their smiles shine from some deep inner core.

"I'll go for the explanation first, if you don't mind, Mrs Hamilton, you see I'm rather..."

"Curious, yes I see that in you, clear as day. Right," Mrs Hamilton continued, "first an explanation as to why I selected this room. This was the old earl's study and very few people were ever admitted. It was his sanctuary, really, complete with dusty books and faded wallpaper, just the way he liked it." Mrs Hamilton looked shrewdly at Maeve for a moment, trying, Maeve thought, to make up her mind about something. "It was young Lily's favourite room in the castle as well," she added, clearly having decided that Maeve probably knew about the origins of Pudding almost thirteen years earlier.

"Lily Morrison?" Maeve asked, her confirmation of Mrs Hamilton's meaning gaining another of those enlightened, light-full smiles.

"They often came here to be alone. The dowager countess never, to my knowledge, came down this passage to seek out his private room. But that's not the reason I asked you to come here today, Lady Strathfulton. Fi believes I owe you an explanation about Mr Hamilton, God bless him, and I tend to believe her in this incidence."

She cleared her throat and began at the beginning.

"My dear husband has not had an easy life, more so in recent years, I'm sorry to have to tell you."

"Mrs Hamilton, if it's about where your husband is right now, I do know, if that makes it easier."

"A great deal easier, because the indignity follows me around everywhere. But, it was me who should have been a guest of His Majesty."

"Really?"

"Well, not strictly, but I put terrible pressure on the poor man to restore our fortunes and, if my husband is guilty of fraud, I do believe I put him up to it."

"If?"

"Well, that's the thing, Lady Strathfulton." She paused then. Maeve could see the physical effect of her summoning up her moral strength to carry on. "My whole life has been a lie with me pretending to be something I am no longer."

"You mean aristocracy?" Maeve was about to say that it's not all it's cracked up to be and perhaps she was better off without it, but Mrs Hamilton corrected her, saying:

"Not the aristocracy, but a family of wealthy landed gentry."

"I see," Maeve said, although she didn't see at all clearly and felt a need for peace and quiet to ponder the situation, doing what her police training had taught her so she could see the situation from every angle. "Now, am I right in saying that your dislike of Mr MacGregor was not solely because of your worries about Fi?"

"Hole in one," she said.

"I beg your pardon."

"With that last statement you've driven off the tee and managed the wind enough to bear down on the green, so, Lady Strathfulton, I would like to confirm your view that my distaste for Mr MacGregor was compounded by Fi's friendship with him, but that was not the origin."

The origin, as Maeve soon discovered, was the deep suspicion that Mr MacGregor had played Mr Hamilton, like a cat might do with a mouse, setting him up as the fall guy in case the scheme he had devised to defraud the Strathfulton estate didn't pan out.

"Which it didn't," Maeve confirmed, "because of a bright young police officer somewhere in the chain of command who realised that the old earl couldn't have signed over the farms when he was in custody himself."

"Do you realise what this does, Mrs Hamilton?"

"Yes," she replied, solemnly, "it puts me, and to a certain extent Fi, right in the frame, which is daft because there's no other supporting evidence, but I'll happily take on that risk if it means a chance to pull my family back together."

Far away from them, they heard the distinctive bang of the gong for lunch.

"We must get back, Mrs Hamilton." Mrs Hamilton didn't reply in words, but went to the door and opened it wide for her countess to pass through.

And, a moment later they had slid back into the hall to see Fi, Kat and Angus urging the five thousand into the state dining room, only used on special occasions.

But, there was no sign of Mrs Morton. Maeve looked towards Fi, hoping for an exclamation. That's when she noticed Fi dressed identically to Kat in their best uniforms. A moment later, the fully-confessed Mrs Hamilton looked ready to murder someone as she took in the sight of her daughter clothed as a maid.

"Mrs Morton said she had to be away, with her husband being so ill, and she asked me to fill in for her," Fi said by way of explanation when Mrs Hamilton and Maeve, acting as a pair, cornered her a few minutes later.

"But the uniform?"

"She ordered it for me, she said so I could be like Kat."

That's when the cloud started lifting and Maeve could see daylight again; just the most modest break in the sky at first, but it was progress after what seemed like an eternity in which nothing made sense.

"I need to see Mrs Morton," she said.

"No," Mrs Hamilton replied, "first things first, Lady Strathfulton. You're the hostess at this lunch party and it's imperative that you play your part."

"I'd much prefer that you..."

"No," Mrs Hamilton said and that was that.

The lunch party for one-hundred was as close to a disaster as could ever be imagined. Mrs Morton was doubling as cook generally, but she was nowhere to be found and, it seemed, had done only a little towards the preparations. Instead, Kat and Fi descended to the kitchens determined to do something with the raw fish, meat and vegetables waiting in the larder. Meanwhile, Angus circled the table pouring out wine for all those partaking, rushing down to the cellar for another half-dozen bottles before repeating the procedure all over again.

With the empty bottles mounting on the sideboard, and Maeve wondering whether the cellar could possibly hold any more bottles, Mrs Hamilton suddenly rose, excusing herself quietly.

Maeve waited until the state room door had closed behind her, before standing herself, noting how the gentlemen stood each time a lady left the table.

As it should be.

"I'm just doing a little spying," she said to a giant moustache sitting on her right. She couldn't understand what he slurred back but could tell it was genial.

Thank the Lord above that the Strathfulton cellars were well-stocked. There might be no money in the bank, but there would always be a bottle to hand somewhere.

Back in the hall, there was no sign of Mrs Hamilton. That had to mean she had taken the back stairs; nobody could cross the hall in the few seconds she had on Maeve, nor was there time to climb the main stairs and disappear into the bedrooms above. Logically, she had to have taken the only route that would cover her tracks and that meant heading for the green baize door and the route to the back parts of the house.

But, would she have gone up, down or straight on the level?

Maeve paused a second, before heading down the stairs, guided not by intellect but by instinct.

She was dead right. Although it took her a few minutes to find her way to the kitchen complex. Several turns later, the narrow passage opened up to a large pleasant room dominated by a stove that must have cooked breakfast for Robert the Bruce, rumoured to have stayed at Strathfulton Castle, just that Maeve wasn't sure which century that had been. She just knew he had made friends with a spider in a cave and lived to be king a long time ago.

There were three people at the stove and two of them were arguing furiously.

"Mrs Hamilton," Maeve called after the moment it took to process the scene before her.

"Lady Strathfulton, what are you doing down here?"

"Looking for you," she replied, realising her mistake as the words tumbled out.

"Oh, so you thought I was up to no good, did you?"

"I was... um... just..."

"Mummy, don't be difficult with Maeve," Fi said, risking extending the argument they had been having into a new direction.

"So, it's first-name terms now, is it?"

"Only when we're alone," Fi said, thrusting her largish chin out which involved tipping her head back so she was almost staring at the ceiling. "I made a mistake in calling Lady Strathfulton Maeve, that's all."

"Mrs Hamilton, perhaps you can tell me what you're doing down here in the kitchens," Maeve said, anxious to move the discussion on before sparks flew.

"It was clear to me, Lady Strathfulton, that we would be a long time waiting for lunch and rather than have you deal with a collection of drunken Highlanders with no food inside them, I thought to come down here and help to do something about it."

"We were doing fine without you, Mother," Fi said, almost sulkily. Meanwhile, Kat was just stirring something in a huge pot, not knowing what to say or do with her betters scrabbling and fighting around her.

"I just came to offer my help," Mrs Hamilton said in a sudden effort to defuse the situation, "and I'm sorry, Fi and Kat, for being snappy and commanding."

"That's alright, Mother," Fi replied immediately, actually stepping forward and hugging her mother. Maeve, with her observance training from the police force, couldn't help noticing that Mrs Hamilton's blouse caught a severe dose of some liquid from Fi's apron, but decided not to mention it for the sake of the harmony Mrs Hamilton had just secured with her humble apology.

Ten minutes later, they had the makings of a meal. Mrs Hamilton and Maeve helped them carry the steaming cauldrons up to the pantry that served the state dining room, then left for their places, while Kat and Fi prepared to take around endless helpings of mackerel pate, followed by mackerel roasted in a liberal dose of herbs with potatoes cut very small so they would cook quickly. After that, somehow, they had cobbled together a pork stew which Maeve thought actually tasted like pork stew.

"Mrs Morton has surpassed herself today," several of the guests said as they raised their glasses one more time while Angus wandered around the room; clearly the fumes of the alcohol he had been serving had gone to his head.

Chapter Nineteen

After a lunch that everyone exclaimed to be a raging success, the party splintered off into groups. A lot of the men congregated in the billiards room where a huge man with a curtain of a kilt in a bold tartan Maeve had never seen before, started a knockout tournament, while a small slight man in a tan suit ran a book, pronouncing odds which seemed to take little account of natural ability, and even less of the individual's sobriety levels. Maeve looked in, watching and wondering for a while, then went to the drawing room in search of Fi.

She had the layout of the main rooms downstairs pretty well ordered in her mind now. She felt she could navigate from billiards room to drawing room with ease and there she would find Fi along with Mrs Hamilton and a collection of the other lady guests.

On the way, however, she bumped into Kat carrying a large and terribly hot pot of coffee. The girl looking so frail and dainty that Maeve took the pot for her and carried it to the drawing room.

"Anybody for coffee?" Maeve called, then called again in a louder voice because she got no response the first time around.

There were several takers, which they handled as a team with Maeve pouring the coffee and Kat offering sugar and cream laid out on a silver tray that also bore the cups. Maeve glanced up and saw the concentration on Kat's face and a wave of affection came over her.

There were many questions about the household, the estate, the village, the school, the murder. But, running through this myriad of mysteries was one constant. Maeve knew that whatever else happened, she could always count on Kat.

"Thank you, milady," Kat whispered as they dealt with the caffeine demand together. Then, with a sigh, she added that it was quite tough working at Strathfulton Castle.

"Why's that, Kat?"

"Oh, I didn't mean to complain, milady."

"I don't see it as complaining, not in the slightest. I just want to know any problems you face and then we can work out how to solve them."

"Well, milady, if I'm honest..."

"I want you to be totally honest, Kat. What's worrying you?"

"It's just..." but at that moment, Mrs Morton entered the room with a second pot of coffee, no steam rising from this one, informing Maeve it followed the Strathfulton tradition of serving hot drinks cold, a tradition she could well do without.

Mrs Morton offered it around the drawing room, but received very few takers. Maeve watched her for a few minutes, feeling incredulity rising like a barometer, except, she corrected herself, because the barometer in the hall of her family home rose to indicate fine weather ahead, and the incredulity she aimed at Mrs Morton spoke more of a storm coming.

When she turned back to Kat she saw just the empty space where Kat had been standing.

Meanwhile, Mrs Morton placed the coffee tray on a side table, marched over to Maeve and said in a far too loud voice that this was work for a maid not a housekeeper.

"I poured the coffee just now, Mrs Morton," Maeve replied, "so it's fine for a countess to pour, but not the housekeeper to the countess?"

"That's not what I meant, milady." She left the room, her too-loud words lingering in the cold air, despite the early summer sunshine outside.

There really was a storm coming.

Except, thinking of storms, Maeve's attention was drawn to the garden, and to Fi, clippers in hand, tackling some strange shrub Maeve had never seen before coming to Scotland.

Leaving the babble of forty voices behind her, she stepped out of the French doors, instantly feeling the fresh but warm air on her shins. The sunshine on her back and face from the south felt good, making her glad to be alive.

Glad to be a countess with thirty-thousand acres to explore.

"Fi," she said, "what are you doing?"

"Cutting out the deadwood in this rowan," Fi replied, looking briefly at her friend and employer, then back to the task at hand.

"You don't want to chat with the other ladies in the drawing room?"

"I'd prefer to be outside, doing something useful."

"Well, I'm going to drag you indoors, not to the drawing room but to the library where I want to show you something."

"Of course, Maeve, you're the boss." But, the clippers were placed down reluctantly.

"It's not that bad, Fi. In fact, I think it might interest you." Maeve sensed she was dragging her friend away from a passion for gardening. "It's actually to do with the gardens here and some plans for restoration," she added.

"Yes, coming right away, Maeve. Do you know what you want to achieve?"

They chatted about plans all the way to the library, where Maeve pulled out some old sketches and plans she had discovered a couple of days earlier.

"Here, you see," she said as she rolled out a similar

parchment to the one Lily Reid had used to record the Strathfulton and Baritone family tree.

"Are these...?"

"Yes, I do believe they are the original garden design drawn up under the seventeenth earl in... It says the date somewhere, ah, yes, in 1746."

Fi was so engrossed she actually shuffled Maeve out of the way and took central stage in front of the document. "This is fantastic," she said after taking in the details for several minutes, "truly fantastic. Do you think, Maeve, there's any chance we could restore the gardens back to their past glory?"

"I don't see why not, Fi. There's lots more drawings and layouts in the folder I found this one in. Maybe we can take a few minutes and lay them out on the table to see what we're facing."

They did exactly that, finding detailed plans and beautiful sketches of what the now overgrown gardens had once been like.

"This is your true passion, isn't it, Fi?" Maeve said after forty minutes.

"Yes, it is, but I really want to help you get the affairs in order too. I sometimes wonder, Maeve, whether you might allow me to do both, dividing my time between secretarial and gardening duties?"

"I think that would be no more than reflecting reality, Fi, so I certainly give it my blessing."

That, Maeve reflected, was a wonderful thing about being a substantial landowner; it gave you the ability to grant wishes, to spread happiness, like a fairy godmother might.

"There is one thing I would discuss with you, though," she said, remembering the puzzle around the character of Mr MacGregor.

"Your wish is my command," Fi said, not realising how closely her joke brought her to Maeve's thoughts on fairy stories.

"It's a delicate matter," Maeve started, "concerning the man you loved."

"I thought it would be," Fi replied, but offered no more.

"I... eh, I wanted to understand his character."

"I see." Fi said no more for a few minutes, leaving Maeve to take the awkward question forward.

"Some people have spoken about him in a... well, an unflattering way."

"Oh that," Fi replied, "yes, I quite agree."

"You agree?"

"Yes, Ian wasn't a nice person, Maeve. He loved me, I know that, and I..."

"You what, Fi?" Maeve put every ounce of gentleness into her voice and Fi looked up into her eyes in gratitude.

"I thought I was in love with him. He bowled me over, so to say. But Mother and I had a talk this morning about Daddy."

Maeve could see the tears waiting behind her eyes, ready to pour out. This remarkable young girl was only just holding on.

"She told me things about Daddy. That he's not away on business but in another place altogether. She told me also that Ian MacGregor put him there, busy scheming away to enrich himself at other people's expense. I'm ashamed, because I thought I was in love but he was a monster, just using me to try and get land and money. I don't even know if Daddy did anything wrong or whether it was all Ian behind the scenes."

"But, he left you all that money?" Maeve had shifted her chair to be right next to Fi, arm around her shoulder.

"No, even that was a lie. I received a letter from his solicitor this morning. Mother showed it to me. He did make me his heir but there was nothing to leave to me."

"Oh." But Maeve immediately sensed that her verbal response wasn't the slightest bit appropriate. Instead, she leant forward and hugged her tightly, not letting go for over a minute.

"I know it looks bad," Fi said after crying and eventually wiping her eyes, "both Mother and I must seem like murderers to you."

"Not in the slightest," Maeve replied.

"You mustn't just say that, Maeve."

"I wouldn't, Fi. I really wouldn't. If I thought either you or your mother was guilty, I wouldn't be here because I'd be down at the police station trying to get some sense into that silly PC Clarke."

"Oh, you'll never manage that, Maeve, that would be like getting pigs to fly!" Maeve smiled at Fi's joke, thinking she was bouncing back a little already.

"We better get along to the others before they send out a rescue party," Maeve said, standing in order to pack away the old garden plans. "What's this one?" she said, noticing a folded set of papers in amongst the others. She opened it and sat back down with a gasp.

"What is it?"

"It's about the school," she said, reading as she spoke. "It's a deed of gift for the land and buildings that make up Strathfulton School. It's a gift from one of my predecessors to the trust that runs the school."

"So? Everybody knew that the land was Strathfulton land."

"Yes, but look at clause 3. If the school ever closes down the land and buildings revert to the Strathfulton estate."

"So, that means you will own it when it closes? Not Mrs Morton?"

"Mrs Morton?" Maeve asked incredulously.

And then it all made sense. Not just the finances, but everything.

Chapter Twenty

They were back in the drawing room in a jiffy.

"Excuse me, ladies," Maeve put on her best Sergeant Morgan voice to attract attention, "this is a matter of some urgency. Has anyone seen Mrs Morton?"

"Not since she served that almost cold coffee half-an-hour ago," one of the tweed-skirted ladies replied, the others nodding in agreement. "She didn't seem altogether there," the lady continued, "she mentioned that her husband was ill and I wonder if that was distracting her."

"No doubt it did distract her," Maeve replied, trying to think where else to look, thinking also for reinforcements.

Robert Munro. Why didn't she think of him earlier? Last seen an hour ago in the billiard room.

"Quick, Fi, to the billiard room. No, better still, you check the kitchens and then meet me in the billiard room. I'll find Mr Munro and brief him on the latest discovery."

"Of course, Maeve, but why?"

"No time." Maeve was gone, rushing down the uneven corridor that led to the back of the house and the billiard room, tripping several times on the edge of the flagstones, forcing her, eventually, to slow down.

But, how much time did they have? Why hadn't she put things together before this? What was wrong with her powers of reasoning? Had she shed them in accepting life as an aristocrat? Too many questions and no answers.

Correction, there was one answer and that was to the central question of who killed Mr MacGregor.

She thought she knew, but had one more question to ask. And a castle of two-hundred rooms to search, with a thirty-thousand-acre estate beyond that.

Give the man his due, Robert Munro grasped the salient points as if arguing a matter of life and death in court.

"I understand," he said, "the murder you were originally accused of... schoolteacher... school closure... deed of gift. Yep, I've got the picture. We need to confirm facts."

"Yes," said Maeve, just as Fi entered the billiard room where most of the guests had taken to lolling in the easy chairs, old leather monstrosities, or else opening the window and climbing out to the pretty courtyard outside that seemed to have no way in or out, other than through the windows of the adjacent rooms.

Such was the higgledy-piggledy nature of the castle constructed in stages over eight-hundred or more years.

Robert Munro had had his share of drink while waiting patiently for a meal that had turned out to be a lot better than expected, but he was far from the worst and a remarkable sobriety came back to him as he considered the facts relayed by Maeve.

"We must search the whole castle," he said.

"With three of us? That would take a month of Sundays."

"There are three of us, but plenty of them." He indicated towards the mass of sprawled bodies, then launched himself up onto the billiard table and cleared his throat ready for the speech of a lifetime.

"Friends, Romans and Countrymen," he started, then broke into a series of coughs, splutters, snorts and hiccups. "I don't remember the rest, but we need every man still standing." He looked around at their relaxed poses. "No, I take that back, we need every man to be standing. This is an emergency. We have a housekeeper to find, namely one...?"

"Mrs Morton," Fi added, while Maeve was staring open-mouthed at the man on the billiard table.

"Yes, Mrs Morton is missing and Mrs Morton needs to be found. Who's with us on this quest?"

The roar was deafening, much like at the rugger matches at Cardiff that Maeve had attended as a little girl, because everybody in Cardiff watched the rugby. In fact, they said that rugby caused more marriages, births, divorces and deaths in South Wales than anything else, including the coal dust from the mines.

Maeve held out her arm so that Robert could haul her up onto the billiard table to stand beside him.

"Seriously," she cried, gaining silence and attention almost instantly. "We need to apply a little bit of order to this." But, how could it be done? She had it; the vast majority of the men before her would have fought in the war. "I want everybody on parade, come along now, three ranks." Old men and younger looked blankly at her. She made herself even taller, shoulders back, chin jutting out. "Look lively," she cried, "last man in place is a dodo."

She wondered whether she would achieve the order she needed from the chaos that prevailed. Men, when drunk, can become violent, but these were all beyond that, besides not prone to violence in the first place. Beyond drunk is maudlin and that's exactly what they were now, milling around bumping into each other, apologising profusely before backing away and starting the routine all over again.

But, as she stared at them in as imposing manner as she could manage, a shape began to form. At first just a hint that melted away again, but, yes, it was there.

Three lines with fifteen drunken souls in each line.

"Party," she cried, thinking that is what they were – a great big party, "party, wait for it, party, shun!" Forty-five pairs of shoes moved with a differing degree of snappiness to meet the other leg, while ninety arms fell into place at the sides of the bodies.

This was working.

"Party, I want one line searching the back of the house, the second the front and the third are headed downstairs for the kitchen." She then named them line one, two and three.

"What about the female of the species?" came a question when Maeve took the briefing one step further and asked if there were any questions.

"I'm going there to organise them right now. They will search the upper floors and report back to me directly. You're to report to..." she hesitated, not sure of what rank Robert may have made during the war. "Captain Munro," she said, thinking he must have been reasonably junior as he looked well under thirty-five a decade later.

"Spot on," Robert said, grinning like the drunken man he was.

It was a lot easier to mobilise the ladies. In fact, the only real difficulty was in keeping them quiet long enough to pass on the requirements.

"Fi is the first line for reporting," she said once she had got the mission across, "make sure you pass any findings on to her."

"Not me? Said Mrs Hamilton as the meeting broke up. It wasn't said with rancour in the slightest and Maeve was not offended in the slightest.

"I have a special task for you, Mrs Hamilton," Maeve replied, "I want you to search the passage leading to the old earl's study."

"Consider it done, Lady Strathfulton."

"Take one person with you, just to be safe. No, not Fi, she's too valuable to me here in HQ."

· · ·

With close to a hundred people searching, including both of the semi-retired gardeners roused from their afternoon nap, there were cries across floors and up and down staircases. Somehow, Lord Throck managed to get stuck in an attic that no one had been into for years, but couldn't get back down again until the gardeners found some rickety ladders, the shorter of which became a sloping stretcher for a noisy, belching lord of the realm.

With all those people searching, it was Kat who came up with the best lead.

"I meant to say earlier, milady, how noisy it is in our bedroom with the Mortons shouting and yelling all night long. Fi just drifts off but it keeps me awake half the night."

"Show me your bedroom," Maeve said, then stopped and sent Robert in another direction. "I know the Mortons' rooms on the top floor have been searched several times," she said, "but please humour me on this, Robert." She gave particular directions and had Fi as the runner between the two positions.

The bedroom Kat and Fi shared was very small and very plain. Two iron bedsteads, a wardrobe and a chest of drawers with a washbasin on top, plus a pair of bedside tables with a lacy cloth on each one. Maeve told Kat to lie down on her bed and to wait quietly, as if drifting off to sleep. She pulled out her pocket watch and counted off the seconds to four o'clock.

The deadline came, the deadline passed, not a sound was heard.

"That's funny, milady, because I definitely heard the two of them arguing long into the night."

"Could it have been someone else?" She knew it couldn't, because short of ghosts, there wasn't anybody else around, other than old Angus, who usually fell asleep in an armchair in his pantry.

There were rooms upon rooms on the servants' bedroom wing, just none others occupied.

Maeve turned this over in her mind. There was almost always a perfectly good explanation for the inexplicable. She just had to find it. Freddie Blythe would have found it, or Miss Cess Pitt, the centre of Freddie's world. Lady Darriby-Jones had a collection of people around who could assist with working things out.

Maeve had yet to build that circle, but now, more than ever, she knew she would. It might take a few years of give and take, but she would get there. She felt the feel-good things inside her rising up. It gave her tired mind more energy and she went over the whole last few days all over...

"Hidden rooms," she said, jumping up from Fi's bed that they had both gravitated to.

"You mean like a secret passage?"

"Yes, Fi, I bet there are some secret rooms known only to the Mortons. After all, the whole castle is a maze."

"Stay here, Kat. You're ordered to stay in bed. Is that clear?"

"Yes, milady," said with a grin and yet another curtsey.

. . .

Maeve took Fi back down one set of stairs and over to the other set that led to the Mortons' rooms, where Robert was found gently snoring on the sofa.

"Robert, wake up, man. We've got to find a secret way into another set of rooms that either connects with the servants quarters or lies along the back of the rooms on this side of the passageway. First, we need to get our bearings."

The Mortons had a bedroom, a bathroom, a sitting room, kitchen and dining room, along with a tiny study. The whole formed an oblong in shape with one side longer than the other; Maeve couldn't remember the correct geometrical term for a rectangle with one sloping side.

The layout of the rooms ruled out the bedroom, bathroom and kitchen, so they divided the work up by room, Maeve taking the tiny study built into that sloping wall.

"We're looking for a lever or a catch, anything that might lead to a moving panel or a hidden hatch or door."

"Right-ho," said Robert, still very much under the influence, yet proving himself time and time again.

The study was beautifully tidy, everything put away and everything seemed to have its place. An in-tray sat on the wooden desk, an inkwell and a row of pens and pencils, together with a few other incidentals. The wall that faced towards the servants' bedrooms was clean and bereft of any indication that there might be a secret door hidden in there. The opposite wall was covered by the desk, the window dominated the far wall and the door the near one.

It wasn't the study. At that moment, Fi, then Robert, both called the all clear for their respective rooms. It seemed that there was no way forward with this secret door theory.

She went back out of the door to the study, heading for the sitting room where Fi waited for her.

Except, could there be? The wall between study and sitting room seemed extra thick. She closed the study door to look behind it. There was a stopper half-way up the wall to prevent the door banging against the plaster. She wiggled it with her finger and a whole section of wall moved in, revealing a new passage between the rooms they had been searching. Maeve called for electric torches and soon all three were walking warily into the unknown.

Chapter Twenty-One

They found two people in the secret rooms behind the Mortons' flat. The first was dead, the second alive, but only just.

Mr Morton was hanging in the first room they came to, his face purple, his body sagging, feet swaying gently, maybe because of a draught from the chimney. Every few seconds, his feet lightly touched the stool that had, in all likelihood, been kicked away from underneath him. His hands had been tied incredibly securely; there would have been no boyish last-minute escape from danger with hands tied so very tightly.

They moved on through a series of rooms, all dusty and unused, until they came to the last, which was very different. Made out as a bedroom, it had a rather grand bed that dominated the room. To the right, as they looked at it, swung the second person, trying frantically to gain a foothold on the bed.

"It's Mrs Morton, she's alive," shouted Fi, jumping onto the bed and holding the legs to take the weight off the housekeeper's throat. She gasped and groaned as Robert, also standing on the bed, tried hard to undo the rope and lower her onto the bed.

Maeve ran back to the top of the stairs and called for someone, anyone, to get the police. By the time she returned, she could see the pallor of death on Mrs Morton's white skin.

"Why?" she asked the dying lady.

"Because of him," she croaked in reply, a slight nod indicating her husband, "wanted fresh start, no money... only way to buy land at school... buy school and sell. Working well." She paused there, clearly unable to last much longer.

"Why Mr MacGregor?" Fi asked, her voice sounding so young amongst the death that surrounded them.

"He found out... blackmailing..." She sat up suddenly, turned to look at Maeve and said, "stole from you to pay him, so sorry..."

"You know the school reverted to me if closed down, don't you?" Maeve said.

"Yes, but old earl would... sell anything. I bought land around... several plots and fields... my ticket out."

But, Maeve thought as the old lady lost her lingering grip on life, she ended up getting another ticket out altogether, one which was far more final.

. . .

Death in a Classroom

They all knew she had died, but the doctor arrived shortly to confirm it, noting suicide on the death certificate. He left and they waited for the police to come, finally hearing that PC Clarke was last seen going fishing and DI Cassidy was too far gone at the bar of the Strathfulton Hotel to be of any use to anyone.

"It seems like they need a good detective up in these parts," Robert said. "With your background, you might fit the role perfectly."

"Well, as long as I have a good lawyer to see me through the tricky times," Maeve replied with a laugh. She liked the man who clearly liked her. But, going back into the police force, albeit one several hundred miles to the north of her old haunt in the Oxfordshire Constabulary, was not an option. She had loved being in the police, rising to the challenge of early promotion to sergeant, but she had moved on.

She was an aristocrat now and that brought huge responsibilities, ones she rather relished getting to grips with, especially now that she had Fi by her side.

Pudding too, and her mother.

"I think I've got enough on my plate with running the estate, Robbie, don't you think?"

Wait a moment. When had Mr Munro become Robbie? Presumably by way of 'Robert'?

"Yes, Maeve," he replied, "you see tit for tat on names. I was only joking, really. I think you're going to be a first-class countess, exactly what the doctor ordered for this sick and neglected estate."

"Now you're being silly."

"No, I mean every word. By the way, what are you going to do about losing your housekeeper? Young Kat can't do everything, you know, not in a house this size."

"Oh, I know exactly who I'm going to ask and will do so first thing in the morning."

"Who? Anybody I know?"

"Well, you'll just have to wait and see," she replied, laughing as she teased him.

In fact, she didn't go first thing in the morning because another crisis arose when Mrs Hamilton knocked on the door of the morning room at ten minutes to eight the following morning, just as Maeve was rehearsing her recruitment speech in front of the mirror.

"I'm sorry, Lady Strathfulton, I see you've got your hat on so you must be going out. I'll come back another day."

"No, Mrs Hamilton, I can go later. You look as if you have something on your mind."

She did have something on her mind, that being a planned move away from Strathfulton. Mrs Hamilton wanted to apologise for taking Fi away when she had only just started working for Maeve.

"I just cannot afford the rent and must move in with my

sister, although that will be a little hard to endure at times. We haven't always seen eye to eye."

"What about some alterations that might allow you to stay?" Maeve said after hearing the sorry tale.

"Lady Strathfulton, we only have a small income. Plus Fi's salary, of course. The house we have is lovely but the rent is more than we can afford."

"Fi's two salaries."

"Two? I don't understand."

"She gets her salary as my private secretary, as you know. I had a word with her last night about the gardens because her true passion is gardening. She's going to do both jobs. Two jobs means two salaries. She will be head gardener and my secretary, won't she just?"

"But..."

"No, Mrs Hamilton, I'm quite decided and because I'm now an aristocrat, I've become used to getting my way. Seriously, the estate needs people of the calibre of you and your daughter and I think we will all be much the richer for your continued presence."

"But..."

"No more 'buts', Mrs Hamilton. Fi can work out a schedule to repay the back rent and I'll accept whatever is reasonable and affordable. If I'm to make a success of this estate, I need you and your daughter very much on my side."

. . .

The recruitment mission was only thirty minutes delayed and Maeve took the car, rather than walking, getting Fi to come along with her. First, she allowed a few minutes for her mother to explain the good news about staying.

Maeve waited several rooms away from the Hamilton ladies, but was sure she heard a whoop and a holler from Fi, who was smiling broadly when she came to find her employer, twice over, a little while later.

"Where are we going, Maeve?" Fi asked, skipping down the steps and across the drive to the motor car they had borrowed. They would need their own, but first she had to get a grip on the finances of the estate.

"On a recruitment drive for a new housekeeper," she replied, "and I have the perfect candidate. Can you drive to the police station please, Fi?"

Twenty minutes later, Mrs Ritchie, the police station cook and cleaner, and a merry old soul too, stepped into the car with Fi holding the door open for her.

"I'm delighted to accept, milady," Mrs Ritchie said, "who would ever have thought it possible that me, a Ritchie, should become housekeeper at the castle?"

"If you make it half as cosy as my involuntary stay at the last establishment you looked after, I shall be thoroughly pleased," Maeve said, noticing the pleasure she brought to the old lady's face and rather liking her power to do so.

The End

Afterword

Thank you for reading *Death in a Classroom*. I really hope you enjoyed reading it as much as I had writing it!

If you have a minute, please consider leaving a review on Amazon or the retailer where you got it.

Many thanks in advance for your support!

Death in a Prison Cell

Chapter 1 Sneak Peek

The telegraph boy, it seemed, understood exactly what to do. Knowing Mrs Hamilton to be away staying with her sister in Edinburgh (her sister having been foolish enough to marry a lowlander), he came straight to the castle to find Fi, her daughter, now employed by Maeve, Countess of Strathfulton and Baritone, to be her secretary and head gardener combined.

Fi and Maeve were together in the new business room that Fi had set up, requiring her two ancient gardeners to leave their beloved roses for a while and spend a couple of days moving a mass of papers from various locations to the somewhat spare, and sparse, sitting room on the ground floor of Strathfulton Castle.

"This way, we shall have all the correspondence and records in one place, Maeve," Fi had said, demonstrating the flexible nomenclature arrangements the two friends had. When alone, it was always 'Maeve' and 'Fi', Maeve becoming 'Lady Strathfulton' in company and Fi sometimes being referred to as 'Miss Hamilton' when others were around.

"Your choice of room is interesting," Maeve had commented, thinking it typical of her friend to take the room that stuck out at one end of her new home, such that it had views to the south, west and east over the once-glorious gardens that Fi had committed to getting back into some form of order.

Maeve considered it the best of luck with her sudden inheritance of two earldoms in Scotland upon the execution of Lord Barry Baritone for murder, an exercise she, as a police sergeant had played a role in, not having the slightest inkling that she would inherit. That had meant a Welsh girl becoming a major landowner in Scotland where the accent was so strong it felt like a different language.

Good luck comes in threes, so they say. Her second bit of good news was coming across Fi Hamilton. Only seventeen, she had an extraordinary character that gave without counting the cost, combined with a true ability to organise. Maeve had given her the post of secretary out of feeling sorry for the disgraced Hamilton family that was down on its luck, but had quickly come to recognise her remarkable skills, plus her passion for gardening.

The third bit of good luck was financial, and the meeting they were sitting through was one example of this. Her predecessor, Baritone, had been perpetually short of cash, but that was primarily because, so it now appeared, he did not know where to look. There were pockets of opportunity all over the 30,000 acres Strathfulton estate, plus all the mining royalties from the Baritone lands in Ayrshire, firmly situated in the hated lowlands, but still capable of producing considerable income.

Then, as she was learning from this suite of bankers and stockbrokers, there was the trust set up by four earls prior. As a younger son, he hadn't expected to inherit, so had gone to India and made several fortunes. One such fortune had become a trust for the use of each subsequent earl or countess to use for their own private expenditure. One banker, on learning of Maeve's life before as a police sergeant, had rather pompously informed her that he expected the annual income from the trust would cover the entire salaries of all those based at Scotland Yard. Maeve didn't mention that, as a Welsh girl from Cardiff, working in the Oxfordshire Constabulary because they had a tolerable attitude towards female police officers, she had never been to Scotland Yard.

And now, on inheriting and moving to the Highlands, it seems she probably never would.

Maeve thought nothing of it when Angus, the butler, slid silently into the room and whispered something to Fi, who rose from her chair and followed him out of the door; it would be some issue to do with domestic arrangements, the finances for which also fell to Fi.

Mainly because there was no one else capable of doing it. Certainly, Maeve had no head for figures.

The cry broke up the meeting. Who could endure such a piercing scream and continue talking about yields and gains and diversification strategies? Well, it seemed the bankers and stockbrokers could. One of them paused in full flow when the cry penetrated through to the business room from somewhere near the front door, but the moment the cry stopped, despite the thud of something falling to the floor, he continued his monotone. Maeve, however, was moving towards the door, mumbling something about emergencies she didn't quite get the import of herself.

The most worrying thing is she didn't recognise the voice behind the cry. Not that she had had all her staff screaming out loud until she could be sure of the particular tremors and tone of every voice in the establishment, but she knew it wasn't Fi, Kat or Mrs Ritchie, the three that came immediately to mind.

The mystery was solved within seconds; the initial mystery, at least. There on the floor of the hall lay the crumpled body of Fi, dressed in her smart business suit she had been so unsure of wearing, but Maeve had insisted on. She rushed to her new friend, anxious to check she was alright, by which she meant, alive; Maeve had seen too many inert bodies lying where they had fallen.

Except, the cry had most definitely not come from Fi, so there was another element to this mystery she had yet to unearth. But first things first. Was her new young friend alright?

She was, other than a fogginess that made her call Maeve, 'Mummy', but that was understandable.

"Who screamed?" Maeve asked, looking around at the collection of males that had congregated in the hall. There was 'Turtle' Tomkins, the new under butler who Maeve doubted would make the grade to take over from Angus when the time came. Apparently, he was someone's cousin or stepbrother or uncle; that's how it all went on at Strathfulton, favours for those you knew and all that. Angus was unmarried, meaning the long line of Angus butlers would cease when the old man hung up his wine cellar keys for the final time.

"It was Maggie, milady." So, Turtle Tomkins, the slowest servant ever known to the stately home scene, had a voice at least. Moreover, he had been the first to react; perhaps, Maeve considered, she had been a tad too sweeping in her initial view of the man?

"Maggie?" Who on earth was Maggie? "Ah, Maggie, the new girl, is she not?" Maeve answered her own question a moment later. And there she was, standing behind the rude statue, as Maeve called it. Its real name was the 'nude statue' done by some artist living a natural life in the Orkneys, staying on a sheep farm while actually getting a weekly delivery of food from Harrods. She knew all this because Angus had insisted on telling her, delighting in the contradictions and hypocrisy involved.

That was Angus all over, a marvellous collection of contradiction and hypocrisy, proving that it takes one to know one.

But this didn't help with the problem at hand. She quickly established that Maggie had been going about her business with dustpan and brush, a duster in her apron pocket, when Fi had collapsed onto the floor of the main entrance hall. That was when Maggie issued her scream and Maeve could understand exactly why.

After helping Fi to a chair, in fact one of the huge ones a previous earl had brought back from Africa with the back made of warrior shields and the arms fashioned around two spears towering into the air, she asked Mrs Ritchie, who, despite her advanced age, had sprung forward to assist Maeve, to stay with the patient and administer love and attention in equal doses. That left her free to determine more about what had happened. A quick overview of those present indicated the telegraph boy standing in the open doorway, the telegram still in his hands.

"Is that for Miss Hamilton?" she asked, fearing the worst about her father. He was serving three years for fraud and prison wasn't the healthiest of venues for a late middle-aged man.

"Yes, eh… milady, only it's rightly for Mrs Hamilton, but I knew she was in Edinburgh so I thought to bring it straight to where I knew Miss Hamilton was, milady."

"You did well, boy. What does the telegram say?" What news, indeed, could cause Fi to collapse like that? Maeve feared the very worst.

"Well, that's the thing, you see. I don't rightly know on account of it hasn't been read yet, milady."

The strangest of occurrences, that a telegram should cause such disruption before it is even read?

"You better let me read it," Maeve replied and the boy complied, handing it to Maeve, who turned aside as she opened the telegram:

URGENT. STOP. CONCERNING MR HAMILTON. STOP. CELLMATE FOUND DEAD. STOP.

MURDERED. STOP. MR HAMILTON BEING QUESTIONED. STOP. SUGGEST IMMEDIATE VISIT. STOP.

———

Get your copy of this gripping murder mystery at all good retailers.

A MAEVE MORGAN MURDER MYSTERY

DEATH
in a
PRISON CELL

CM RAWLINS

Also By CM Rawlins

A Lady Darriby-Jones Mystery Series

The Mystery of the Polite Man (Book 1)

The Mystery of the American Slug (Book 2)

The Mystery of the Back Passage (Book 3)

The Mystery of the Murder that Wasn't (Book 4)

The Mystery of the Miss Cess Pitt (Book 5)

The Mystery of the Bag of Bones (Book 6)

The Mystery of the Sudden Demotion (Book 7)

The Mystery of the Missing Misses (Book 8)

The Mystery of the Royal Rogue (Book 9)

The Mystery of the Mothering Sunday (Book 10)

The Mystery of the Christmas Crackers (Book 11)

The Mystery of the Wettest Wedding Ever (Book 12)

The Maeve Morgan Murder Mystery Series

Death in a Classroom (Book 1)

Death in a Prison Cell (Book 2)

Death in a Distillery – COMING SOON

Death in a Very Small Place Indeed – COMING SOON

Death on Ben Strathfulton – COMING SOON

Newsletter Signup

Want **FREE** COPIES OF FUTURE **CLEANTALES** BOOKS, FIRST NOTIFICATION OF NEW RELEASES, CONTESTS AND GIVEAWAYS?

GO TO THE LINK BELOW TO SIGN UP TO THE NEWSLETTER!

https://cleantales.com/newsletter/

Printed in Dunstable, United Kingdom